Horse Soldier's Return

Bounty hunter Horse Soldier returns from Navajo country to find his wife, Sarah, and daughter, Clementine, have been taken by killers Cal Livermore and Tod Ridelle. But the kidnappers don't want money: they want Horse Soldier, in revenge for the shooting of Laramie Pete Livermore.

Horse Soldier teams up with Running Deer McVicar who is in pursuit of his father's killer but can they rescue Sarah and Clemy in time?

Horse Soldier's Return

James Del Marr

A Black Horse Western

ROBERT HALE · LONDON

ISBN 978-0-7198-0823-4

Robert Hale Limited
Clerkenwell House
Clerkenwell Green
London EC1R 0HT

www.halebooks.com

Typeset by
Derek Doyle & Associates, Shaw Heath
Printed and bound in Great Britain by
CPI Antony Rowe, Chippenham and Eastbourne

CHAPTER ONE

When Horse Soldier drew close to his ranch in Texas he
sensed that something was wrong. When a house is empty
it seems to cry out silently that there's no one at home.
That was no big deal; his wife Sarah and his daughter
Clementine might have been away in town. After all Clemy
was at school in Simm City some five miles away and Sarah
rode in with her most days, except that the sun was riding
high and Sarah should have been home by now.

Horse Soldier was a bounty hunter. At least he had
been. He had bought the modest-sized ranch from what
he had earned from bringing in dangerous criminals,
dead or alive. Alive if he could, but often dead. He had few
scruples about tracking down a dangerous gunman and
killer. Horse Soldier had a strong sense of duty. And it had
been a profitable business, too.

His last assignment was in the Navajo country where he
had gone to bring in Hawkeye Hank, alias George James,
and possibly to find a stash of gold. As it turned out,
Hawkeye Hank had settled down and married a Navajo
woman. When Horse Soldier caught up with him the two
had forged a kind of friendship and so Horse Soldier had

given up the idea of bringing him in and there had been no reward.

This had been a matter of honour.

As a bounty hunter Horse Soldier had spent much of his time on the trail and was seldom at home. Sure, he loved his wife Sarah and his daughter Clementine, but he had not been a good husband; maybe he regretted that.

What he called a ranch was really not much more than a farm with a few cows and a flock of hens. It was tucked down in a surprisingly fertile valley. and Sarah had worked hard to make it a home. She was a fine independent woman who knew how to take care of herself. A good match for Horse Soldier himself. They had met when he was working as a wrangler on a ranch in Kansas. It wasn't love at first sight, but a kind of mutual respect that had blossomed into something more. Horse Soldier couldn't have been more pleased with the union.

Perhaps he was thinking just that as he approached the spread and realized the cabin was empty. Where could Sarah be, he wondered?

A bounty hunter has to be cautious: you never knew just who might be lying in wait for you. So Horse Soldier reined in close to the cabin and dismounted. He took his Winchester from its scabbard and approached the door which was creaking gently in the breeze. That in itself was suspicious and weird. So he pushed the door open with the muzzle of the Winchester and peered inside.

Not a sign!

'Anyone at home?' he called.

Not a sound.

He walked right in and saw something strange immediately. On the table lay two half-empty breakfast plates as if

6

Sarah and his daughter had suddenly leaped up and left the building without a sound. Like being summoned to Heaven or Hell by the Dark Angel, Horse Soldier thought with a shiver of apprehension and a jolt in his stomach.

What could have happened to Sarah and Clemy? Just as he was on his way home, too. He had telegraphed ahead, so he knew they were expecting him.

Then he saw the ragged note held down by a mug. He took it up and slid out the paper and saw that it was in Sarah's handwriting, though a bit more scrawly than usual.

Hallo, Horse, it said. That in itself was suspicious. Sarah never called Horse Soldier 'Horse'. He had always been Mike or Mick to her, usually Mike. The note continued: *When you get home, I won't be here. I've gone away for some time. So please don't follow. When I'm good and ready, I'll be in touch again.*

The note was signed *Sarah*. Horse Soldier had never called Sarah, Sarah. It had always been Sar. Another matter for suspicion.

Horse Soldier sat down at the table to consider things and the truth suddenly fell on him like a thunderbolt from the sky: Sarah and Clementine had been kidnapped!

He reached for his Frontier Colt and laid it on the table between him and the door just in case someone came in to gun down on him.

He hadn't been sitting there for more than a minute before he heard a rider approaching, so he took up the Colt and cocked it. Someone was close to the door. Then the door was thrust open and a man appeared.

'Don't shoot!' the man said raising his hands.

'Ed!' Horse Soldier said, lowering the Colt.

7

It was Ed Potkin, his neighbour who lived just half a mile away. Ed was looking perplexed and worried. 'Saw you ride in jest now,' he said in a creaky hillbilly tone. 'Thought I ought to ride over and see how you are.'

Horse Soldier was on his feet. 'What's going on, Ed?'

'That's what I was wondering, Horse,' the old rancher said. 'Didn't know you were expected back. Saw Sarah and Clemy with a whole bunch of riders come sun-up this morning.'

'A whole bunch of riders?' Horse Soldier asked him. 'How many would that be, Ed?'

'Oh, maybe six or seven,' Ed replied. 'Kept my head down in case they see'd me. I was danged surprised, I can tell ye, Sarah being such a keep-to-yourself person an' all.'

Horse Soldier handed him the note. 'Read that. There's the answer, Ed.'

Ed produced a pair of antique spectacles and perched them on his nose. His eyes popped. 'What does this mean?' he asked.

'I guess it means Sarah and Clemy have been kidnapped.' Horse Soldier said.

'My Gawd, you're right!' the old rancher gasped. 'I knew those riders were up to no dang good.

'What can we do?' Ed asked.

'I'm not sure,' Horse Soldier said. He had faced many difficult situations but this was entirely different. His own family were under threat. After a moment, he said, 'Will you do something for me. Ed?'

'Of course. Anything. Anything at all,' the old man replied, in his squeaky tone.

'I wonder if I could ask you to look after the ranch for a few days? Would that be all right?'

8

Ed shook his head vigorously. 'Of course. Me and Phoebe will do anything we can.'

'Just milk the cows and collect the eggs, that sort of thing. I don't want you to get yourselves involved too deep here. It could be dangerous.'

Ed was looking at the paper again. 'It says here: "*When I'm good and ready I'll be in touch*". So what do you aim to do?'

Horse Soldier nodded his head thoughtfully for a moment. 'I'm going to ride into Simm City, that's what I'm going to do.'

'Well, if that's what you want. And don't you worry none about the ranch. Phoebe and me will be only too glad to oblige.'

Horse Soldier didn't know quite why he was riding to Simm City but he had always been a restless spirit and he could never settle down until he had made up his mind to do something.

Simm City was no sort of a city at all. One of the old pioneers, a certain Samuel Simm, had established it a half a century back and called it his city and the name Simm City had stuck. It was just a collection of buildings: a general store, a couple of saloons, a small school, a livery stable, and, of course, the sheriff's office.

When Horse Soldier rode in nobody took much notice of him. He was just another dust-laden rider riding down Main Street which was main street only in name since it was just about the only street in the so-called 'city'.

He made straight for the school and tapped at the school-house door. When he went inside the children were all seated behind their desks with their slates in their

9

hands. Mrs Beardmore, the teacher, was dictating to them. Mrs Beardmore had been the teacher for what seemed centuries. Nobody had met her husband and it was assumed that he was either dead or had vanished. She had a very good memory and when she looked up she recognized Horse Soldier immediately.

'Why, Mr Millar!' she said. 'How is Clementine? Is she sick?'

'I'm sorry to break in like this,' Horse Soldier apologized. 'I've just got home this morning and I wanted to ask you when Clemy was last in school.'

'You mean she isn't at home?' Mrs Beardmore asked in some dismay. 'She didn't come in this morning so I thought she must be sick.'

Horse Soldier glanced at the children and saw they were all looking at him with various expressions of curiosity and apprehension. 'Sarah and Clemy have gone missing,' he said to Mrs Beardmore quietly.

'Oh, dear!' Mrs Beardmore said in alarm.

Horse Soldier could see from her expression that she was thinking all kinds of things and the kids were picking up on it too.

'Thank you, Mrs Beardmore.'

He turned and made for the door. As he left he heard a babble of voices and Mrs Beardmore saying, 'Don't worry, children. I think Clemy has gone on a short vacation.'

The sheriff was sitting in a rocking-chair by the door of his office. Occasionally he flapped a fly away with an old newspaper. When he looked up he saw Horse Soldier staring right down at him and his bushy eyebrows shot up in surprise.

'What can I do for you, mister?' he asked.

In his black Stetson and his dark vest, Horse Soldier might have been a hold-up man about to rob the bank. You never knew what to expect when a stranger rode into town. Sheriff Stafford was new to the job. He had come from further east. So he had no idea who Horse Soldier was.

'Do you happen to know Sarah Millar?' Horse Soldier said.

The sheriff looked a little alarmed. 'Why Sarah! Of course I know Sarah. She has a small ranch about five miles out from here.'

'Well, I'm her husband. Name's Mike Millar but everyone calls me Horse Soldier.' The sheriff thrust his paper aside and rose from his rocking chair. 'Why sure, I've heard of you.' He stuck out his hand. 'Sheriff Stafford. Good to meet you, Horse.'

Horse Soldier accepted the hand and it felt like a slice of dead ham.

'So you just got in from wherever you've been?' the sheriff said uneasily. Horse Soldier saw that his eyes shifted about without settling on anything or anyone in particular. He was not a man to be relied on.

'I just got in,' he said, 'and I find my wife and daughter have gone.'

'You mean like gone?' Sheriff Stafford asked.

Horse Soldier offered him the paper that Sarah had written. The sheriff accepted it as though it was some kind of insect that might sting. Then he screwed up his face and began to read. 'I'm afraid your wife and daughter have left you,' he surmised.

'My wife and daughter have been kidnapped,' Horse Soldier said with decision.

Sheriff Stafford looked right and left down Main Street as though searching for the missing wife and daughter. 'That's too bad, Mr Horse Soldier,' he said. 'That's too bad.'

Horse Soldier stepped in closer. 'Like I wanted to ask you something, Sheriff.'

'Sure, sure,' the sheriff said uneasily.

'I guess you must keep your eye on things in Simm City.'

'Why sure I do! That's my job,' the sheriff said more confidently.

'Then you must know whether you have seen any strangers in town lately.'

The sheriff screwed up his features and stroked his prickly chin. 'Well, yes,' he said, 'a stranger did ride in earlier this morning. I believe he's in the Simm City Saloon right now.'

Horse Soldier touched the tip of his Stetson. 'Thank you for that, Sheriff,' he said.

'If there's anything I can do,' the sheriff said, 'I'll be glad to oblige. I mean about Sarah and young Clemy. She's a right friendly girl, that daughter of yours.'

'Must take after her mother,' Horse Soldier said, as he swung into the saddle and turned towards the saloon which was across the street no more than 200 feet away.

When he pushed back the door everything was strangely still inside, so still you could hear a fly buzzing around and tapping against the window pane. Stan Balding, the bartender and owner was sitting low behind the bar sipping his usual beer. The only other person in the saloon was a swarthy-looking guy who might have been Mexican or half Indian. As Horse Soldier entered the bar

12

the man looked up at him with keen searching eyes.

'Well, I'll be darned, if it ain't Horse Soldier!' Stan Balding exclaimed. 'You just got in from your travels, Horse?'

'Something like that,' Horse Soldier said, and he ordered a beer. 'Make it a large one,' he added.

'Sure thing!' The bartender poured out the beer.

Horse Soldier had been watching the stranger and he noticed that as soon as he heard the word 'Horse' he leaned forward with keener interest.

Stan Balding liked to hear the latest gossip but, before he could ask the next question, Horse Soldier moved away from the bar and sat at a table with his back to the wall, facing the stranger.

The stranger was still scrutinizing him closely. Now he nodded slightly and a faint smile came to his thin lips. 'Did I hear right?' he said in a quiet but determined tone.

'That depends what you heard,' Horse Soldier replied.

'Thought I heard the man call you Horse,' the stranger said.

Horse Soldier paused. It was difficult to tell whether the stranger had a gun strapped to his hip since he was behind the deal table, but he guessed he might have. The stranger could easily make a move and shoot at him from under the table, but life was a matter of chance, so Horse Soldier just sat there with his hand on the butt of his Colt shooter.

'That's right. Most people call me Horse Soldier. That's come to be my name.'

The stranger nodded again. 'There can only be one Horse Soldier and that's the man I'm looking for.'

Horse Soldier tensed. Was this some kind of emissary

13

sent by the *hombres* who had kidnapped Sarah and young Clemy?

'So it looks like you found him,' he said between his teeth. 'Now, what can I do for you, mister?'

The stranger got up from behind his table and moved forward with his hands spread in a gesture of peace. 'Mind if I join you, Horse?' He glanced at Stan Balding whose ears were pricking up like ass's ears. 'I don't like for everyone to know my business.'

'Just as long as you keep your hands away from that hog leg of yours, you're welcome.'

The stranger pulled out a chair and sat down opposite Horse Soldier. He offered his rather large hand and Horse Soldier examined it suspiciously.

'Who are you?' he asked quietly.

'I don't think you've heard of me, Horse. My name is Running Deer McVicar.'

Horse Soldier grinned. 'Running Deer McVicar,' he said. 'Sounds like an Indian name.'

'That's because I'm half-Indian, half-Scot,' Running Deer said with a hint of pride. 'My old man was a Scots hunter. They called him Squaw Man, but that didn't worry him none. My ma was Kiowa.'

Horse Soldier took the offered hand and gave it a squeeze. Running Deer's grip was neither too firm nor too soft and flabby; there was something determined and direct about it.

'So you've heard of me?' he said.

'Sure, I've heard of you. I know you're a bounty hunter and you've brought in a whole bunch of killers. That's your business.'

'How d'you know where to find me?' Horse Soldier

14

asked him.

'A man makes enquiries,' Running Deer replied.

Horse Soldier pondered for a while. 'OK, Running Deer, what do you want of me?'

Running Deer seemed to relax slightly. 'Let me explain. A year ago a bunch of men broke into my pa's place. You see, he had a stash of gold in the cabin. He never liked banks. Didn't trust them nohow.'

'You mean they stole the gold?'

'Worse than that. My pa never gave in to nobody. So he brought out his shotgun and gave them a blast. He brought down one of them but the others gunned down on him and stole the gold.'

'You mean they wounded your pa?'

'No, they killed him, blasted him right to Hell, or maybe to Heaven, depending on your point of view.' Running Deer was looking right into Horse Soldier's eyes with an uncomfortably steady gaze 'You see what I'm saying to you, Horse?'

'Well, not exactly,' Horse Soldier replied. 'I guess you didn't come all this way to tell me a sad story about your pa.'

'That's right,' Running Deer said. 'I've come to you because I want you to help me in finding those killers so that I can blast them to Hell like they blasted my pa, and in this case it must be Hell as sure as I'm sitting across this table from you.'

That gave Horse Soldier something to chew on, just as he was about to retire and take things easy on the ranch, too.

Running Deer was watching him closely again. 'I can offer you good money,' he said quietly. 'We track these killers down together and I give you a good reward. It would be generous, probably the most generous reward you've had from your bounty hunting so far.'

Horse Soldier laughed quietly to himself. 'If you know who these killers are why don't you track them and kill them yourself?'

Running Deer nodded. 'Listen, Horse, I'm offering you a partnership here.'

'A partnership in what?'

Running Deer paused. 'You come in with me, I'll cut you in on a ranch I own in New Mexico. I'll sign the deal fair and square before the notary. How would that be?'

'That would be fair enough if I'd seen the ranch,' Horse Soldier said. 'Only I have a little difficulty of my own, right now.'

'What would that be?' Running Deer asked him.

Horse Soldier took a gulp of his beer and told Running Deer that his wife and daughter had been kidnapped and so far he hadn't received any kind of demand from the kidnappers.

'Then what are you doing here?' Running Deer asked him. 'What the hell can you do if you don't know who's holding them?'

Horse Soldier had to admit that he didn't know the answer to those questions.

'Tell you what, Horse,' the other man said, 'Why don't we do a deal? You help to track down my pa's killers and I'll help you track down your wife and kid's kidnappers?'

Horse Soldier paused for a second but what had he to lose?

'I think we can do a deal on that,' he said, stretching out his hand.

16

They rode back to Horse Soldier's ranch. After all, if the kidnappers wanted to make contact and claim a ransom, they would know where to look.

As they approached they saw Ed Potkin faithfully tending the livestock. 'So you've come back, Horse,' the old man said in his creaky tone.

'It seemed a good idea,' Horse Soldier said. 'That way they know where to find me.'

The old rancher straightened up. 'No news, I guess.'

'Nothing to speak of, except that Clemy wasn't at school and nobody's seen the kidnappers. That sheriff is about as useful as a blind bat at a Sunday bazaar.'

Ed Potkin gave a high snigger. 'You're right about that and he's about as useful with a gun as a blind bat, too!' He went off into a wheezy laugh and then suddenly stopped as though he realized this kidnapping business was a serious matter. He was eyeing Running Deer with suspicion.

'This is Running Deer McVicar,' Horse Soldier introduced.

'How do, Running Deer,' Ed said, holding out his hand.

Running Deer gripped the proffered hand.

'Running Deer will be staying in the barn tonight,' Horse Soldier explained. 'We have a little business together,'

Horse Soldier was beginning to trust Running Deer, but a man could never be too sure. When he had suggested the barn Running Deer had made no objection. In fact he seemed pleased. 'Good idea,' he had said. 'Anyone sneaks up on the place we can look out for one another better that way.'

Now Ed Potkin was smiling and shaking his grizzled old head. 'Now, why don't you two gentlemen come up to my place this evening for a bite of supper? My good woman Phoebe would be glad of that. We don't often entertain visitors and she'd give you a damned fine meal. Dumplings are her speciality. She does them real good.'

'Thanks, Ed, but I think we'll stick around down here for tonight,' Horse Soldier said. 'I can rustle up some chow. It won't be much but it will have to do.'

'Well, if you change your mind you can come up later,' the old man said.

He stopped at the doorway and turned and shook his head. 'Well, dang me, I forgot,' he said. 'It was important too!'

Horse Soldier looked at him and waited.

'I was out there tending the beasts,' the old man said, 'and I happened to look up and saw two riders. I couldn't describe them, but I knew they were watching me. So I pretended I hadn't noticed them and I just got on with what I was doing. After just a short minute they turned and rode away in that direction.' He pointed to a low bluff not far from the ranch.

Horse Soldier and Running Deer exchanged glances.

Running Deer narrowed his eyes. 'Up there, you say.' He pointed towards the bluff.

'A little to the left by that itsy bitsy bush up there,' Ed Potkin said.

Running Deer turned to Horse Soldier. 'Why don't we take a look see?'

The two rode up to the the bush that Ed Potkin had indicated and Running Deer looked down at the ground where the tracks were still visible. Then he dismounted and examined them more closely.

'What do you see?' Horse Soldier said.

'I see like the man said: two riders close together looking down at your spread.'

'You think you could track them?' Horse Soldier asked him.

Running Deer screwed up his face as he looked down at the tracks. 'I might track them if the weather holds,' he said. 'But there's something kind of strange about these tracks. Two things, in fact.'

'Two things?' Horse Soldier repeated. Was Running Deer some kind of medicine man? he wondered.

Running Deer was nodding. 'First thing is these two riders did nothing to cover up their tracks. The land is dry. It's like they wanted you to follow them.'

Horse Soldier could see the tracks quite distinctly. If the rain kept off even a man with half an eye could follow them. 'Sure they want me to follow them,' he said. 'I think it's a kind of invitation. I guess those *hombres* who are holding Sarah and Clemy want me to follow them. You know what that means?'

Running Deer was nodding again. 'I get the picture. They want you to follow them because they're more interested in you than your good woman and the child.'

'That's exactly what I was thinking,' Horse Soldier said.

Running Deer looked up and sniffed the air. 'Well, they chose a bad time. There's going to be a storm and real soon too.' He was looking over at the hills where dark clouds were beginning to climb up and mass like fevered giants.

'You're right,' Horse Soldier said. He wanted to get after those two riders immediately, but he knew that would be a bad policy; however much he wanted to rescue his wife and daughter, he mustn't rush into a quick decision and endanger their lives even more.

19

'What's the other thing?' he asked Running Deer.

Running Deer was on his knees examining the tracks even more closely. 'You see that?' He pointed to one of the tracks. 'And there it is again.'

Horse Soldier got down and stared. He had done a deal of tracking himself but Running Deer was a lot better. 'What do you see?' he asked.

'I see a distinctive mark on those tracks,' he said. 'You see that one there?' He pointed to a slight indentation in one of the hoofmarks. 'And there it is again.' His finger pointed to another of the tracks.

Horse Soldier looked more closely. Yes, those two marks were distinctive. Not many people would have noticed, but Running Deer was quite a skilled tracker.

Running Deer straightened up. 'Well, that's like the workings of fate, Horse,' he said with a grin.

Horse Soldier wasn't a great believer in fate but he looked at Running Deer, waiting for him to explain.

The man continued to smile. 'Those hoofmarks are the same as one of the *hombres* who came after my old man,' he said. 'That means our paths had already crossed before we met in Simm City. Now isn't that kind of weird?'

Horse Soldier didn't smile. Could this be some kind of trick? he wondered. 'Yes, that's weird,' he said.

'Well, I knew I'd come to the right man,' Running Deer said. 'It seems we've forged a kind of partnership here.'

They might have speculated further but now there was a loud rumbling in the sky and those threatening clouds were getting ever closer. In another minute there would be thunder and lightning and a deluge of rain.

So they turned their horses and rode back to the ranch. Before they got there, however, the rain started and they decided to take shelter in old man Potkin's place. Phoebe, his wife, welcomed them with open arms.

'Come in, Horse, and welcome,' she crowed. She was delighted to see them. The Potkins had few visitors and Phoebe was a people person and she loved to cook and complain about life. Though Ed Potkin was a social person as well, it was nice to see someone different.

'Make yourselves at home and join us for a bit of supper,' Phoebe said. 'And I'm real sorry to hear about Sarah and Clemy. You think it might be some kind of misunderstanding, Horse?'

Horse shook his head grimly. 'That's no misunderstanding, Phoebe. Those *hombres* have their own plans. I guess they're out to get back on me.'

Phoebe looked alarmed. She was a stout and friendly person like her husband. Although she wasn't too bright her heart was in the right place.

Horse Soldier and Running Deer were glad to accept a good supper with Phoebe's excellent dumplings, As they sat down at table, the heavens opened and the rain came down like hammer blows.

'What will you do?' Ed Potkin enquired.

'I guess we'll take it one step at a time,' Horse Soldier replied. 'I think we've got a big problem here.'

There was bright flash of lightning and Phoebe gave a scream.

Horse Soldier could see Running Deer's face illuminated. It looked sort of yellow and green but Running Deer didn't flinch: he was nodding in agreement. The storm rolled on.

CHAPTER TWO

Some miles away in a hidden valley there was an old two-roomed cabin. Though it appeared to be ramshackle like a drunken man about to collapse and die, it was much sturdier than it looked. Inside there was a bunch of men and two women, one of whom was just a girl. The woman was Sarah Millar, Horse Soldier's wife, and the girl was Clementine, his daughter. Sarah was a fine, attractive woman of about thirty-five and Clementine bore a strong resemblance to Horse Soldier, though she had a sweet and trusting face.

As the storm rolled through the hills, Sarah held her daughter's hand and squeezed it to reassure her. 'Don't worry,' she said, in a quiet contralto voice, 'the storm won't do us any harm.'

'Why have they brought us here?' Clemy asked apprehensively.

'Because they have a grudge against your father,' Sarah told her.

'Does that mean we're in danger?' Clemy asked.

'Not if we're careful,' Sarah said. That wasn't really true and Sarah knew it, but she needed to work out her strategy. She wasn't a woman to sit down and accept her fate.

On the other hand she must protect Clemy and make sure she was safe.

They weren't alone in the room. There was a man with a dark beard sitting opposite them and he was listening to everything they said. Sitting half in the shadows, he looked to Clemy like the very devil himself. Clemy was just eleven years old and she found it difficult to understand their situation.

The man with the beard spoke in a rather sinister crackly tone. 'You don't need to worry none about a thing,' he said, 'just as long as you obey the rules and do as you're bid.'

Clemy thought things over. 'You mean we've been kidnapped?' she asked.

The man with the dark beard paused for a moment. 'I wouldn't put it like that, missy. I don't think you're here for money, though money would be useful,' he said with a chuckle.

Sarah knew it wasn't about money. It was about revenge. A man who brings in gunslingers dead or alive for reward takes a big risk, and so does his wife and child.

'You know what, mister,' she said, 'keeping us here isn't going to do you any good at all.'

The bearded man continued to chuckle and it sounded like sandpaper drawn across rough metal. 'I think it's for us to decide on that,' he said. 'Me and the boys, that is.'

Sarah could hear the so-called 'boys' arguing and guffawing in the room next door. Possibly getting drunk too. Though she hadn't seen her husband Horse Rider for months, she could picture him clearly, a hard but just man, always restless, forever trying to work out the solutions to things, especially dangerous things. Right now he would be trying to figure where they were being held. And what would he do then? she wondered.

Sarah didn't mind too much for herself but she was deeply concerned for her daughter Clemy who was an intelligent and sensitive girl, and Sarah wanted the best for her.

'So what are you going to do with us?' Clemy asked pertly.

Maybe she didn't sound as frightened as she felt because the man with the beard said, 'You got a lot of grit, girl. Where does that come from, your pa or your ma?'

A look of defiance flashed across the child's face. 'I get it from both my pa and ma,' she said.

'Well, that's good for you, I guess,' the man said with a grin.

Clemy was watching him closely with a look of quiet assessment. 'Did you ever meet my pa?' she said.

The man looked startled and then he ran his hand through his bushy beard. 'Can't say I have,' he said. 'I heard of him, of course. I know he's good at shooting people.' He chuckled quietly again. 'Do you happen to be good with a gun yourself, missy?'

'I've never tried, 'Clemy admitted, 'but I guess I might if I had to.'

'That's a good spirit,' the man said. 'Just as long as you don't point it in my direction.'

'We don't talk about guns,' Sarah intervened sharply. She was always thinking of a better future and she wanted her daughter to be brought up as what she thought of as a lady. On the other hand, she could see the sense of talking politely to the man with the beard since their lives might lie in his hands and she had heard that, if you humour a hostage-taker, he will sometimes soften and lower his guard eventually.

Only now there was another distraction. From the next room they could hear renewed laughter and shouting and, perhaps, the beginning of an argument.

A man named Cal Livermore was sitting at the plank-top table drinking from a bottle. In fact, he wasn't drinking, he was sipping. A bottle in Cal Livermore's hand was always something of a prop. He held it up and and sipped occasionally but he never drank much. He used the bottle to point at people and thump on the table occasionally to make his point. In fact, Cal Livermore was a hard character who worked out his moves as much as he could in advance. In that respect he was like his brother, Laramie Pete Livermore, who had died at the hands of Horse Soldier up at the Sweet Spring in the Badlands close to Hawkeye Hank alias George James's place.

That was why he was here. That was why they were all here, all seven of them. Except for Mingo who was in the next room watching over the women, and Daryl Fabre who was on guard under the broken-down ramada outside, they were all in the dilapidated room in that tumbledown shack.

Apart from Mingo and Daryl Fabre and Cal Livermore himself, there were four other *hombres*, some of them sitting at the plank top table and the others lounging around in the room. Each one of these men had one thing in common: they wanted revenge for something Horse Soldier had done to their kin. Either that or Cal Livermore had bribed them with the promise of a deal of money.

'That was a neat job,' Spike Ovenwood said. 'You worked it out just good.' He spoke in a somewhat over-flattering tone that didn't do too much to please Cal Livermore, who preferred men of determination to flatterers.

'Yeah, finding the right place and getting hold of the two females was OK,' Vic Ridelle acknowledged. He was cousin to Tod Ridelle who had also perished up at the Sweet Spring. 'But what's our next move? That's what I want to know.'

Cal Livermore ran his hand over his dark cadaverous chin as though meditating on when he should have his next shave. 'I've got that all worked out,' he said. 'But first I'd like for you to tell me what happened, Vic, when you went down to that piddling little cattle shed of theirs they call a ranch.'

The men sitting round the table guffawed with derisory laughter which is what Sarah heard from the next room.

'Well now, me and Charlie here rode up to look at the place like you said. There was an old man working there and it sure wasn't Horse Soldier. He pretended he hadn't seen us but we knew he had.'

'That's right,' Charlie Springfield said. 'So we hung around like you said, keeping ourselves under cover. And then just before that storm blew up two *hombres* rode up to the bluff. I saw them through my spy glass just as clear as I can see you.'

'You say two?' asked Gus Daniel. He was the last of the seven and he usually spoke last as well.

'That's right, two,' Charlie said, 'and another thing: I know who Horse Soldier is, of course. Everyone knows Horse Soldier. But the other one. . . .' He paused for effect.

'OK, what's the big drama?' Gus Daniel asked.

'Well,' Charlie said, 'to tell you the truth I was surprised. It was like sort of fate, you know.'

'Fate!' Gus Daniel scoffed. 'Cut out the mystery, Charlie! Just give us the facts.'

'Well, you know what? The other guy was Running Deer McVicar,' Charlie said.

There was a stunned silence.

'Who the hell is Running Deer McVicar?' Gus Daniel laughed.

Cal Livermore decided to intervene. 'You remember we did that job with the old geek up Winslow way. He had a stash of gold in the place and we decided to go for it. He blasted us with a shotgun and we had to shoot him dead to get the gold.'

'So?' Gus Daniel said.

'Well,' Cal Livermore explained. 'I happen to know that Running Deer McVicar was in fact, that old geek's son.'

There was a moment's silence and then they all leaned forward or sat up.

'You mean Horse Soldier and Running Deer McVicar have thrown in together?' Gus Daniel asked.

'It begins to look that way, don't it?' Cal Livermore said.

Spike Ovenwood gave a snigger. 'That means we got two for the price of one.'

'That means you get two slugs in your gut instead of one,' Cal Livermore said, contemptuously.

'What's with this Indian, anyway?' Gus Daniel asked.

'What's with him is he's Kiowa on his mother's side and Scot on his father's side and he's done a deal of tracking. Worked as a scout for the army one time.'

27

That caused another thoughtful silence.

'That means we have two *hombres* to kill,' Vic Ridelle speculated.

'That's no big deal,' Spike Ovenwood chimed in.

Cal Livermore gave him a sharp look. 'Why don't you keep your trap shut, Ovenwood? Save your crowing for the big day.'

Gus Daniel was chewing his lip. 'That Indian tracker breaks up the picture,' he said. 'It means we have to act quickly before they get the upper hand.'

Vic Ridelle went over to the window and peered out. He couldn't see much on account of the grease and dust of ages but that didn't stop him from thinking. 'I don't like this stinking hole, anyway. We stay here, we're like rats in a trap waiting for someone to stamp on us.'

'What do you suggest?' Cal Livermore asked him. Though he liked to be top man he had some respect for Ridelle's thinking.

Ridelle turned from the window. 'The way I see it is this.' He took a step towards the rickety table. 'What we want is Horse Soldier dead. Leastways, that's what I want.'

'That's agreed,' Spike Ovenwood put in again. 'But not before he's curled up and begging for mercy, eh, Cal?'

Cal Livermore made a contemptuous noise in his throat. 'This isn't about dying. It's about suffering. A dead man doesn't feel a thing. He doesn't even know he's dead.' He looked around at the others with a strangely ominous expression on his lined and haggard visage. 'Like the man says, this isn't about death; it's about knowing you're dying and knowing you've lost everything before you die. That man who calls himself Horse Soldier has to feel the pain running right through his body and right through his soul as well. That's what this is about.'

'Yeah,' agreed Ovenwood. 'So that's why we've got his wife and daughter, to make him feel like a piece of bread toasting over a flame. Is that what you mean?'

Cal Livermore pulled his face in a sneer but did not deign to reply.

Vic Ridelle placed his hand on the table and looked down at Livermore. 'If we kill those two women, Horse Soldier is going to wither like a scorched leaf and die,' he said.

'Not before he comes at us with both guns blazing!' Cal Livermore replied vehemently. 'Don't you know anything about men like Horse Soldier?'

'You're dead right on that one,' Gus Daniel said.

'So what's our next move?' Ridelle asked.

'What we do is we send somebody down to his ranch to talk to Horse Soldier. We ask his woman to write a note to him just to show that she and the girl are still alive. Then Mingo rides down to the ranch and drops it in.'

That information was greeted by a kind of meditative silence.

'Why Mingo?' Gus Daniel asked. 'Because he's dumb enough to do it?'

Cal Livermore grinned. 'Because Mingo has sand. And he's curious too. I know he's just longing to meet Horse Soldier and Horse Soldier won't go tough on him because, if he does, we just pop off Mrs Millar and the girl. And another thing: Mingo wasn't in on the Running Deer McVicar job. So McVicar won't be tempted to jump him.'

There was another moment of nervous silence.

'OK, agreed,' Vic Ridelle said after a moment. 'Mingo rides down come sun-up.'

CHAPTER THREE

Come sun-up Horse Soldier and Running Deer were eating chow in the ranch house. Ed Potkin was in the barn attending the livestock. He enjoyed caring for animals and hated slaughtering them when the time came. He even talked to them as he moved among them and he sensed they appreciated it. It wasn't so much what he said, it was more the way he said it and the tone of his voice that counted. At least that's what he figured.

When he looked up through a slit in the barn door, he saw a big bearded man approaching on horseback. So he slid out silently through the door and made for the ranch house.

'There's a man riding in,' he told Horse Soldier. 'Looks like he's alone but you never can tell. Thought you should know, Horse. Big bearded *hombre*. Looks like old Satan's brother hisself.'

Horse Soldier was already on his feet, strapping on his frontier Colt. He turned to Running Deer. 'Keep yourself scarce,' he said. 'Listen and watch and see what you can learn.'

Running Deer wasn't the man to argue with common

sense. So he nodded abruptly and disappeared.

Horse Soldier went to the door of the ranch house and watched as Mingo rode in.

Mingo was nodding and even grinning as he rode up to the place. 'Would you be Horse Soldier?' he asked in a tone that reminded Horse Soldier of a wheel that needed oiling.

Horse Soldier nodded.

'Don't look much like your picture,' Mingo said.

'Don't feel much like it,' Horse Soldier replied. 'Did you want something, mister?'

Mingo sat his big roan and wagged his head. 'I came to tell you your woman and daughter are safe and well. They even send their regards.'

A man with a sense of humour, Horse Soldier thought. 'Why don't you cut out the bullshit and get down to business?' he said.

Mingo nodded. 'Whatever you say, Mister Horse.' He reached into his saddle-bag and held out a a scrap of paper. 'This here is written in your wife's fair hand.'

Horse Soldier stepped forward, took the offered paper, and unfolded it. 'When did my wife write this?'

Mingo held his head on one side like a bird that considers the prospects of being caught in a net. 'Not too long ago,' he said. 'Why don't you read it?'

Horse Soldier wanted to take the paper into the cabin and sit down with it. But he just stared down at it and read it. There was no doubt it was in Sarah's hand and there was a note at the end from Clemy too. That was a relief.

Mingo was still sitting on his horse. 'You see they're both alive and well and they're looking forward to seeing you too.'

31

Horse Soldier glanced up at him and saw that he was smiling but it wasn't a particularly amiable smile.

Mingo nodded again. 'Mighty fine woman you got there, Horse, and that girl of yourn has grit too. They're both somewhat discomforted at the moment, but as I say they're looking forward to seeing you again.' He raised his hand. 'Why don't you read the letter?'

Horse kept himself steady as he read the note.

Hello Horse – not Mick or Mike, he noticed again – *We are both well and we aim to keep well. This man brings our good wishes. If you want to see us, you are to wait up on the bluff and someone will meet you. And when you come, please come alone.* It was signed *Sarah*, not *Sar*. Underneath there was short scrawl that said: *Love you, Dad, Clementine.*

When Horse Soldier had read the note he was tempted to draw his Colt and cover the bearded man and when he looked into Mingo's eyes, he saw that he read his thoughts.

'Don't do anything foolish,' Mingo said. 'Use your head. You want my advice, just do as the woman says. And, by the way, come unarmed and come alone if you want to see your wife and daughter again. It would be a shame to see them led like the sacrificial lambs in the Good Book, wouldn't it? 'Specially with them being such fine women, too.'

As Horse Soldier watched, Mingo touched the brim of his slouch hat, turned his horse and rode away.

Horse Soldier turned and saw Running Deer in the doorway.

'So, what do we aim to do?' he asked.

The picture's getting clearer,' Horse Soldier said. 'Those *hombres* are getting at me through my wife and daughter. The big question is, if I let myself get into their hands, what do they do? Do they let Sarah and Clemy go, or do they kill us all?'

Running Deer screwed up his face in thought. 'That's a tough call, Horse. One thing is clear: those gun sharks aim to get you one way or the other and once you're in their hands you're dead meat.'

That was the stark truth and Horse Soldier knew it. 'That's not the problem,' he said. 'The problem is how do I save Sarah and Clemy?'

'Difficulty is, we don't hold many aces in this game,' Running Deer replied.

'You say *we*,' Horse Soldier said. 'This is about me and my folk. You don't need to be involved in this.'

'Oh, I think I do, Horse! What kind of a rat-trader d'you think I am, anyway? I thought we had an agreement here. You help me and I help you. I'm the extra card you got.'

Horse Soldier looked at him and thought about it. 'That's true,' he said. 'The big question is how we play you.'

'Yeah,' Running Deer agreed. The way I figure it, those skookums probably know I'm around because they've seen me. That big beard told you to go alone and unarmed and that's what you must do for the sake of those two ladies of yourn.'

'Well, that makes sense, but what about you?'

Running Deer looked thoughtful. 'I'm still working on it. What we do is to get inside the heads of those killers and see things from their angle.'

Horse Soldier said, 'That's the easy part: they want me dead, and they're not too particular about killing anyone who gets in the way.'

'That means you're the ace in the hole, Horse.'

'How do you figure that?'

'If you keep the appointment, you and your women might as well be toast and cheese. If you hold back, those women stay alive. They might not be comfortable but at least they're still breathing.'

Horse Soldier was beginning to see the sense in it. 'Then how do you suggest we play it?'

Running Door gave a twisted grin. 'Well, first you don't keep that appointment – I keep it!'

Horse Soldier opened his mouth slightly in surprise. 'Then what?'

'I tell those bags of scum it's no deal unless you see those two ladies and know that they're well.'

'What then?'

'That's the first move. We decide what to do next when we see how they react.'

Running Deer rode up to the bluff at the appointed time and looked out across the rolling plains which were something to see. Horse Soldier was some distance away watching through his binoculars. It had been a tough decision and neither of them had much idea of what would happen next. Running Deer sat his horse and waited like some kind of pop-up figure on a shooting-range, but he had been in tight squeezes before and he had always managed to wriggle out of them somehow. So now he just waited and waited until he saw riders approaching. There were three of them. One was Mingo and the other two were Gus Daniel and the blabbermouth Spike Ovenwood. All were heavily tooled up.

When the three riders saw Running Deer they paused

and stood off a piece. Running Deer waited with his Winchester cradled in his arm. After a moment's hesitation Mingo spurred his horse and rode forward. The two others fanned out on either side like they wanted to spread the target.

'You have an appointment, mister?' Mingo said in a jeering tone.

'Not exactly,' Running Deer said. 'I'm just here taking the air in case someone wants to talk to me. No law against that, is there?'

Spike Ovenwood gave a kind of nervous titter.

Mingo tossed his head and grinned. 'You wouldn't be here because a friend of yourn got chicken feet, would you?'

Running Deer grinned back. 'I don't look at the feet, Mister, I look right into the other man's eyes. That way you can tell if what you see is a skunk or a human being.'

Mingo gave a harsh chuckle. 'So Horse Soldier decided not to come. Is that the deal?'

'The deal is he sent me as his representative, like a friendly lawyer, you know.'

'Mighty fine-looking lawyer,' Spike Ovenwood put in. 'Lawyers carry law books and stuff. You don't look the part exactly.' He gave a peal of high-pitched laughter.

Mingo tossed his head, just enough to let Running Deer see he despised Spike Ovenwood.

'I suppose Mr Horse Soldier realizes he's risking the lives of those two fine women, one of whom happens to be no more than a girl. A pity her life should be wasted on such a lost cause.'

'The game isn't over until the last card drops,' Running Deer told him.

35

Mingo grinned in appreciation. It seemed he was dealing with a man of wit. 'So you've come with a game plan?' he said.

'I've come with a suggestion,' Running Deer replied.

'Well, you make your suggestion and I'll convey it to the right authorities.' Mingo wasn't thrown: he was taking everything in his stride. Running Deer paused to consider matters.

'I'll tell you what you do, mister. You go right back to the big man and give him this message from me. My friend Horse Soldier might be ready to give himself up just as long as he can see his wife and daughter safe and well.'

Mingo nodded and looked at Gus Daniel.

Gus Daniel gigged his horse to one side and spoke for the first time. 'That note the woman sent should be enough for you.'

'Well, that's the deal,' Running Deer said. Now he was looking past Mingo towards Gus Daniel. What he saw was a lean-looking type with a clean-shaven jaw and tight lips. Not a man to trifle with. Daniel rarely smiled. He took himself and life far too seriously. Maybe he was one of my old man's killers, Running Deer thought.

'If anything happens to those two females, Horse Soldier isn't going to like it one little bit,' Running Deer said.

Mingo gave a harsh chuckle. 'Sounds like we're in for a real ding-dongy time,' he said.

'Tell you what, why don't we meet here same time tomorrow and you can bring the two womenfolk.'

'We'll see what the big man says,' Gus Daniel chipped in.

'Don't push your luck,' Mingo advised. He gave a signal and the three kidnappers turned and rode away.

Horse Rider was lying prone on another bluff about a mile away. He held his binoculars steady and watched the whole proceedings.

Do I trust Running Deer? he asked himself. What do I do if he betrays me and throws in his lot with those kidnappers?

The meeting seemed amiable enough. Just one *hombre* parleying with three others. There were no angry gestures and no suggestions of gunplay. The big man Mingo even appeared to be laughing from time to time.

Horse Soldier's patience was like a strung-out piano wire. He was strongly tempted to mount his horse and ride down there shooting the daylights out of them. Yet he kept himself in check and thought about his next move.

Then he noticed something interesting: as the three riders turned their horses and rode away, they didn't bunch together: they split up and rode in three different directions.

They think nobody will know which one to tail, he thought. But all roads lead to Rome. So he picked out Mingo and decided to follow him.

Mingo was no greenhorn. All the time he was parleying with Running Deer he was wondering where Horse Soldier could be. Not in the ranch house, that was for sure. He had more than a hunch that Horse would be concealed up there somewhere, watching the whole proceedings through a spyglass. So what? he thought. If we lead him back to the shack where the woman and the girl are being held, so much the better. Then Livermore and Ridelle have him like a nut in a nutcracker and the females can go.

Mingo had nothing against Sarah and Clemy. In fact he rather approved of women who weren't easily flustered. You had to be tough to survive out here on the frontier and in Mingo's book they were the best of the breed. What would happen when Vic Ridelle and Cal Livermore had blasted Horse Soldier to hell? Why, he himself might step in and claim the bride. Mingo had a yearning to settle down and become a respectable married man and now he saw a way of fulfilling his ambition. He could become a husband and a pa at the same time, especially if he managed to rescue those two females . . . at least that's the way he figured it in his dreams!

So, as he rode along, Mingo's mind was overflowing with ambition. But Mingo was no fairy fancier. He had a sense of fun too. If Horse Soldier was following he would lead him a merry dance, right round the mountain and even towards Simm City itself. Why not? Simm City was as good a place as any to lay up and kill a man.

Mingo had nothing personal against Horse Soldier. In fact, from what he knew of him, he rather admired the man. But business was business and self-interest was self-interest, wasn't it?

Though Horse Soldier had been away hunting villains quite a lot of the time, he knew the country around the ranch pretty well. He had even taken Clemy on rides to pick out the main features for some miles around. There were a number of ruined cabins on the range, the cabins of settlers who had been unable to make a go of it, or who had died fighting the Comanche years back. He guessed that Sarah and Clemy were being held in one of those ruined cabins. But which one? He couldn't be certain.

However, one thing became quite clear: the big bearded man was having a game with him, leading him by the nose. They were going on a roundabout route towards Simm City.

What should he do? It was too late to follow one of the other riders. Either he must follow Mingo to Simm City or give up the chase. After a mile or two he figured that he should follow the bait and see what would happen. It might not take him closer to Sarah and Clemy, on the other hand, it might give him a lead of some kind.

Mingo was chuckling to himself as he rode into Simm City by a side route. He saw Sheriff Stafford sitting on his rocking-chair cleaning his Winchester.

'Hi there, Sheriff!' he said, looking down from his mount.

Sheriff Stafford looked up from his Winchester and gave a flickering uncertain smile. 'Hi there, mister. You just rode in?'

'Why sure. I think I have an appointment.'

'Really! Well, can I help you?'

'Sure.' Mingo smiled down at him. 'Man called Horse Soldier. You know him?'

'Well, I met him, yesterday I think it was. He has a place about five miles from here. Told me his wife and daughter have gone missing. Fine woman Sarah and that Clemy is a real sweet kid, too.' He gave Stafford a quizzical look. 'Is your business something to do with that?'

'Could be,' Mingo said. 'Listen, Sheriff. If you happen to see Horse Soldier around please be kind enough to tell him I shall be in the saloon over there, taking in a beer, or maybe two. It's thirsty weather, you know.'

'Sure is.' The sheriff tipped his hat. 'If I see him, I'll tell him like you said.'

He watched with a slight air of suspicion as Mingo turned his horse and rode over to the saloon.

Stan Balding looked up as the big man entered. 'Howdy, stranger!' he said cordially.

'Howdy, my good man!' Mingo responded. 'Draw me a beer, will you? And make it a big one. I've got a terrible thirst on me.'

'Did you ride from far?' the ever-inquisitive Balding enquired.

There were some dozen men in the bar and the calico queen had just appeared at the top of the stairs. She stopped as though frozen and all the men in the room quietened and looked over at the stranger.

'Far enough,' Mingo responded, with a nod towards the calico queen. 'I'm expecting to meet a friend.'

'Oh!' Stan Balding's sparse eyebrows shot up. 'And who would that be?'

'That would be a man who calls himself Horse Soldier. Real name's Millar.' Although Mingo spoke quietly, every head shot up and the calico queen seemed to shrink back against the stair rail.

'Horse Soldier?' Stan Balding said with his eye on the woman. 'Yes, we know him here. Just got in from his adventures two days ago He has a small ranch some four or five miles from here. His good wife and his daughter have gone missing. Some say she's run off somewhere. Wouldn't be surprised. Horse Soldier is hardly ever at home, ask me.'

Mingo leaned forward on the bar. 'Well, my good sir, I don't think anyone did ask you. So why don't you just draw that big beer and leave me to drink it down?'

One or two of the men at the card table were chuckling quietly and the woman continued down the stairs. Mingo tipped his Stetson and gave her a wink before she disappeared into a back room.

Horse Soldier was riding down what Simm City called Main Street. He was thinking about Sarah and Clemy and he was deeply worried. When Sheriff Stafford saw him he rose from his rocking-chair and said, 'Why Mr Horse, you're just in time for your appointment. That big man rode in some half an hour back. He's biding there in the saloon waiting for you, I guess.'

Horse Soldier nodded and went over to the saloon and pushed against the swing doors. Mingo was sitting at the bar with a large glass of beer in front of him. When Horse Soldier appeared in the doorway everyone in the bar room froze and nobody said a word. Stan Balding opened his mouth and crouched behind the bar, reaching out for a shotgun he kept there in case of emergencies. The calico queen peeped out and then disappeared abruptly.

Then Mingo nodded and grinned. 'Why, Mr Horse, I didn't expect to meet you again so soon. Why don't you join me in a beer? You must be awful thirsty after your long and dusty ride.'

That went some way to relieving the tension. Stan Balding reached out and poured another good measure.

Horse Soldier went over to the bar and took a stool.

'Thought you'd catch up with me sooner or later,'

Mingo said.

'You made it easy,' Horse Soldier observed. 'Like you expected me to follow.'

Mingo took a swig from his glass and sighed. 'You're a damned astute fellow, you know that?'

Horse Soldier never responded to flattery. 'You got something to say to me, why don't you say it good and clear?' he suggested.

Mingo shrugged his huge shoulders. 'I got quite a lot to say to you, Horse, but I don't think here is the best place. Why don't we just quench our thirsts and then go take a stroll.'

Stan Balding was grinning to himself. He was just itching to hear what the two men would say. He laid the shotgun aside and breathed a sigh of relief.

Horse Soldier and Mingo went outside and sat on the edge of the sidewalk, not too close but close enough to talk confidentially.

'I knew you would be watching from up there,' Mingo said. 'I felt it all the time I was talking to that lawyer friend of yours. He said you wanted to see your good woman and your girl before you would do any kind of deal. Leastways, that's what he said. And that *hombre* is one astute fellow. He must be wondering where you went to.'

Horse Soldier shifted slightly on the sidewalk. 'Why don't you cut the crap, Mingo, and get to the point?'

Mingo gave that nasty chuckle of his. 'Well, the point is this, Horse. You want your wife and kid back and I want to help you in that.'

Horse Soldier was looking over at the sheriff sitting under his ramada well out of earshot but watching. 'Why would you want to help me?' he asked suspiciously.

'Well, let me put it like this: I've been guarding those two females and I've come to know them and I've come to admire them too. Those two womenfolk are no shrinking violets. They're women with sand in their craw and they know how to speak up for themselves. I admire that in a woman.'

Horse Soldier was listening intently and he couldn't make up his mind about Mingo. Though the big man spoke reasonable words, there was something behind them that he couldn't quite figure . . . a kind of lilting that was both jeering and jocular at the same time.

'What are you laying out for me?' he asked.

'Well, I know where those two females are being held and I can take you right to them.'

What kind of offer was that? Horse Soldier wondered.

'More than that,' Mingo added, 'I could help you rescue them.'

Horse Soldier's heart was jumping like a jackass, but he tried to keep himself under control. Why should this *hombre* want to help him rescue Sarah and Clemy? *What was in it for him?*

'Maybe it would help if you told me who is holding my wife and daughter,' he said.

Mingo gave a thoughtful nod. 'I thought you might say just that. And I'll tell you the truth. You might remember two names in particular. One is Livermore and the other is Ridelle. Do those names mean anything to you?'

'Laramie Pete Livermore,' Horse Soldier said to himself. 'And Tod Ridelle too.' Of course he remembered. Those were two of the men whom he and Hawkeye Hank had had to kill up at the Sweet Water in the Navajo country. So now he knew why Sarah and Clemy were being held. This was a matter of revenge and he was the target!

'That's the God's own truth,' Mingo said. 'I know exactly where your wife and girl are being held and I can take you there. But there are conditions. After all, a man doesn't want to get himself killed, does he?'

That sounded reasonable. 'What conditions have you in mind?' Horse Soldier said.

'Well now.' Mingo ran his hand through his beard. 'Me and Gus Daniel and that chucklehead Ovenwood had a conference with your sidekick Running Deer as you know because you were watching through your spyglass, and Running Deer, who, by the way, has his own thoughts about this whole business, said you would want to see those two females alive and well before you would make any kind of deal—'

'That's the truth,' Horse Soldier said.

'Then you would give yourself up and take the consequences.'

'The only thing that matters to me is the lives of my wife and daughter,' Horse Soldier said.

'That's what I figured,' Mingo said. 'Just like I would be if I were a husband and father. Only' – he paused – 'in this case it could be different. You could come out of it alive and I could come out richer. You see what I mean?'

'I hear what you're saying, Mingo, and I think I know what you're offering, too.' Mingo was sitting on his right which would make drawing the Colt somewhat difficult. He was tempted to lash out with his fist and drop the big man right off the sidewalk and on to the dust of Main Street and then kick him good and hard. But Mingo was big and strong and he had the gleam of intelligence in his eye.

'You mention riches,' Horse Soldier said. 'What kind of riches had you in mind?'

Mingo raised his head and grinned. 'I guess a few thousand would be enough just as long as we were honourable enough to keep to the agreement.' Mingo read the papers and he had heard of Horse Soldier's reputation for straight dealing.

'That could be arranged.' Horse Soldier said. 'I guess we could reach an agreement on that.'

After the meeting on the bluff, Running Deer watched the three emissaries ride away, each one in a different direction to put him off the scent. Then he searched the other bluff where Horse Soldier was supposed to be watching everything through his binoculars. He expected to see Horse Soldier riding to meet him but nothing happened.

Which of those *hombres* shall I follow? he asked himself. Running Deer was an experienced guide and tracker and he had little doubt that he could pick up on the trail that would lead to the place where Sarah and Clemy were being held. Pick on the most stupid, he thought. So he decided to follow the tracks of Spike Ovenwood.

No big deal! The tracks led through brushwood and soft ground where, after the storm, the horse's prints were clearly visible. Maybe, a little too clearly, he thought.

I'll just ride on a little until I'm sure of the place, then I can mosey back and talk things over with Horse, and we can figure out our next move.

They say you don't hear the one that hits you and right at that moment it came. He didn't hear it but he felt it and, as it came like the slam of a heavy punch to knock him out of his saddle, he asked himselfm What the hell? Why is this stupid thing happening to me?

But it was too late. He was lying on his side and his horse had bolted.

CHAPTER FOUR

Things were getting unbearably hot in the cabin and the stink was terrible. Sarah and Clemy had been in the same room since they had been kidnapped except for the occasional trip outside to relieve themselves. Their stomachs were crying out for food since they had been given nothing but small portions of hard jerky. During her excursions outside Sarah had taken a good look around and she knew exactly where they were. It was the old deserted cabin of that wild eccentric Ross McMee who had died from hooch poisoning some five years back. Though scarcely habitable, the cabin had survived remarkably well since the old man's death but it was not exactly the place to set up home. It was no more than an hour's ride from the Millars' place and Sarah knew that, sooner or later, Horse Soldier would find out where they were.

Now they were being guarded by Daryl Fabre, the guy who had been on watch under the ramada the night before.

Fabre was a big contrast to Mingo. He was a distant cousin to Vic Ridelle and he was in this for the excitement and the prospect of killing. He had heard of Horse Soldier and he was ambitious to have his scalp on his belt or his head on a plate. That way he would be a big man in the territory. He was short and light but he had a big mouth and even bigger ambitions. He hated idleness and resented being ordered to guard a couple of females. Women were nothing but slaves to him.

'You waiting for your pa to come and get you out of here, start thinking again,' he said in a rather high-pitched, crazy-sounding voice to Sarah and Clemy.

'No need to scare the child,' Sarah protested.

'Why not?' Fabre asked. 'She's got to grow up sooner or later, so it might just as well be now.'

Clemy *was* afraid but she had no intention of letting that nasty little man see it. 'My pa is coming to get us out of here,' she said defiantly.

'That's what you think!' Fabre crowed. 'But I've got another story for you. Your pa is on his way to getting himself strung up on that dead tree outside. Dead on dead, it will be. Have you ever seen a dead man hanging wild-eyed and stiff on a gnarled old tree?'

'Of course not!' Sarah said. 'That's a terrible thing to say!'

'Terrible or not, it's the truth!' Fabre jeered. 'It'll be in all the papers. Famous bounty hunter meets his end on a hanging tree! I might do a drawing of it. I'm right good at making drawings. I do all the details like the tongue hanging out and the dead eyes staring out.' He let out a cruel chuckle. 'I could be a famous artist if I put my mind to it.'

'Well, maybe you should choose a proper subject,' Clemy retorted. 'And not try to frighten folk.'

Fabre opened his mouth in astonishment. No child had

ever talked to him like that before. 'Why you!' He stared around in fury and then did the only thing he knew how to. He drew his shooter and held it up as though he was about to beat down on Clemy's head with it.

Clemy gasped and Sarah sprang between them to defend her.

A voice said, 'What the hell's going on here?' Cal Livermore was standing in the doorway with his bottle.

'This man threatened my daughter!' Sarah shouted.

Clemy was crouching on a flea-bitten bed and she was trembling all over.

Daryl Fabre shook his head. 'I was just kidding around, Cal. Nothing serious.' He holstered his weapon.

'Well, you can bring the kid in for some chow,' Livermore said. 'We have things to discuss out here.'

Old man McMee had been ambitious and he had built the cabin with rooms in the hope of getting himself a wife sometime. Unfortunately the hooch had got him instead. Sarah and Clemy were allowed to sit at the litter-strewn table to eat their food. At the other end sat Cal Livermore, drinking out of his bottle, and to his right was Vic Ridelle. Charlie Springfield was outside, keeping watch. Daryl Fabre kept looking out of the cracked window to see what was going on outside. Sarah could see he was a hyperactive individual and his cruelty came partly from that.

They hadn't been chewing on their jerky for more than a minute when Fabre started back from the window. 'Somebody's coming!' he said. 'Looks like Gus Daniel.'

Then they heard the sound of an approaching horse, followed by the voices of Charlie Springfield and Gus

Daniel. Daniel spoke in a quiet murmur and Springfield was questioning him in a much more excitable high-pitched tone.

'Only one of them,' Fabre said. 'I wonder what happened to the other two.'

When Gus Daniel came into the cabin, Sarah could see he was uneasy.

'Well, what happened?' Cal Livermore asked him.

Gus Daniel spoke in a clipped impatient manner. He gave a precise account of negotiations between the three of them and Running Deer on the bluff.

'You mean Horse Soldier didn't show?' Vic Ridelle asked in surprise.

'My guess is he was watching from somewhere close,' Gus Daniel explained. 'Running Deer said Horse Soldier wouldn't do a thing until he saw his wife and daughter were safe.'

Sarah saw Clemy give a start but she kept alert, listening to the conversation.

'He wants to play with their lives like chips in a poker game,' Daryl Fabre put in spitefully.

Clemy looked at Sarah in terror and Sarah squeezed her arm gently, Take no notice,' she whispered.

Daryl Fabre gave a menacing chuckle. 'You don't need to worry, Mrs Horse Soldier, one way or other your old man is dead meat!'

Cal Livermore slammed his bottle down on the table. 'OK, Fabre, cut the crap. What happened to the other two?' he asked Gus Daniel.

'We rode off in different directions like you said. I think Running Deer followed Ovenwood.'

'What about Mingo?' Vic Ridelle asked him.

50

Gus Daniel shrugged. 'I don't know about Mingo but he has plenty savvy so he knows what he's doing.' He paused and creased his brow. 'Only thing is, I heard a shot.'

'A shot!!' Clemy cried out involuntarily.

'Who was shooting?' Cal Livermore asked quickly.

'Couldn't say,' Gus Daniel replied. 'It could have been anyone.'

Livermore and Ridelle exchanged glances. Sarah held on to Clemy's arm to keep her steady and calm though she was almost trembling herself.

Before they could speculate further, Spike Ovenwood rode in at a gallop. He rushed straight into the cabin shouting at Charlie Springfield as he came.

'What the hell!' Cal Livermore and Vic Ridelle sprang up, reaching for their guns.

'Don't worry, boys!' Ovenwood shouted. 'We got one down and one to go. Easy as shooting clay pigeons!' He was full of glee because of his own prowess.

'What happened?' Livermore asked him.

'Well' – Ovenwood swaggered up to the table with his thumbs in his belt – 'that dumb Indian took it into his stupid head to follow me. Of course, I knew what he was up to, so I led him through the brush and gunned down on him.'

'You shot the Indian!' Ridelle exclaimed.

'Best thing to do,' Ovenwood boasted. 'Thought I'd get him before he got one of us.'

Ovenwood expected to be praised but he was in for a disappointment. 'So you shot Horse Soldier's buddy?' Ridelle said. 'And now Horse Soldier won't get Running

Deer's message. We might as well have not had the meeting on the bluff.'

'Waste of time and energy,' Gus Daniel agreed sardonically.

We must get away from here, Sarah thought. If we stay here we're all set to die. She started looking round for something to defend herself with. But then she took hold of herself and started to think. Don't be fool-headed, she thought. Whatever happens I have to make sure that Clemy comes out of this alive.

'We need to get out of here,' she said to Livermore who, she figured, was the most determined of the killers. 'The child needs fresh air.'

'There's plenty out there,' Fabre sniggered.

Ovenwood laughed too; he was feeling mighty proud of having gunned Running Deer – another notch to be carved on the barrel of his Winchester.

Cal Livermore shrugged and gave Sarah what he thought was a gentlemanly smile. 'Why don't you just escort the two ladies outside?' he said to Gus Daniel.

Gus Daniel dragged himself up from the table.

'And don't forget to turn the other way when the time comes,' Livermore added.

Ovenwood laughed again and Fabre gave an evil snigger. 'If'n you're too long out there, Daniel, I'll come out and take a look see. You hear me?'

The two laughed again and Gus Daniel escorted the two ladies outside.

Mingo looked out across the hills towards the ramshackle cabin and he saw Sarah and the girl come out and sit on a bench as Gus Daniel looked around somewhat uneasily, as though he expected trouble and wasn't sure from which direction it might come. A thin spire of smoke rose from the cabin chimney.

Why have I thrown in with this bunch of knuckleheads? Mingo said to himself. Anyone can see that smoke for miles around. That might just as well be saying, 'I'm here for the taking. Come and get me'.

Mingo was uneasy in his head. He knew he was in a strong position but he couldn't make up his mind how to play his cards. He mounted up and rode down the valley towards the old dilapidated cabin. When he got closer, he saw Gus Daniel reach for his gun and Sarah and Clemy look up with their hands shielding their eyes. It was now getting towards sundown and the sun sat like a ripe apricot on the hill. Mingo saw a look of relief on Sarah's face. This handsome woman could be my future wife if I play my hand right, he thought.

'You took a long time,' Gus Daniel said.

Mingo looked down at him and grinned. 'Had to ride in a circle, man,' he said. 'Throw a certain gentleman off the scent. You know what I mean?' He winked at Clemy.

'Have you seen my pa?' Clemy asked.

'Sure I've seen him. He sent his regards to you, too.'

Sarah gave him a hard and bitter look.

'When is he coming to get us?' Clemy asked.

'Soon enough, soon enough,' Mingo assured her.

'Don't play games, Mingo,' Gus Daniel said.

Charlie Springfield had his Colt .44 trailing at his side. He was still theoretically on the lookout but he figured nobody could approach the run-down cabin without being observed. In front the view was unobstructed right up to the hills. The bush behind it was so dense with mesquite that only a creature like the fabled Big Bear could break through.

Mingo went into the cabin to make his report.

'What happened to you?' Vic Ridelle asked him.

'Where have you been?' Cal Livermore said.

'Well, I've been riding around, riding around,' Mingo told him.

'Riding around where?' Livermore demanded.

'Well, you see, Cal,' Mingo said, stroking his silky beard, 'when we went for our parley on the bluff, Horse Soldier wasn't there. He didn't show.'

'We know that!' Ridelle snapped.

'The way I figure it was that Horse Soldier would be skulking close by and he would follow one of us when we split.'

'That makes sense,' Livermore said. 'Are you telling us he followed you?'

'Tried to. So I led him a dance to throw him off the scent.'

'Why didn't you lead him here? That's what we want, isn't it?' Vic Ridelle insisted.

Mingo shrugged. 'That's because I led him into town and we had a drink together.'

'You had a drink with Horse Soldier!' Ridelle said aghast.

'We discussed matters,' Mingo said. 'I led him by the nose like a prize bull. We came to an agreement.'

'What sort of agreement would that be?' Vic Ridelle stared at Mingo in astonishment.

Mingo shrugged again. 'Come sun-up tomorrow

morning, I'm meeting him at that piddling little place he calls a ranch and I'm leading him right here so he can see his woman and child and you can do what you have to.'

'Just like that,' Cal Livermore said.

Mingo nodded. 'Why not? Keep it simple. That's what you want, isn't it? Then you can string him up on that old dead tree out there and everyone will be happy.'

Livermore and Ridelle exchanged looks of wonder. Was this man Mingo a genius?

A man called Morello who was half Spanish was riding through the thicket when he came across a loose horse, all saddled up and grazing at the side of the trail. His own horse neighed a greeting and the wandering horse looked up and tossed its head. Morello knew about horses. He had worked with them all his life in various ranches in the Panhandle and New Mexico. So he just reined in and spoke quietly to the wandering horse. 'What you doing here, horsy *amigo*, and where's your *señor*?'

The horse tossed its head and went on grazing.

'That's some good saddle,' Morello said to himself quietly. 'Could bring in mucho dollars.'

He was about to loosen his lariat and swing it over the stray horse's head when the horse moved on quietly as though it had an appointment somewhere.

'OK,' Morello said. 'You lead, my fine beauty, and I follow.'

But he didn't go far. The next moment he was looking down at a human being lying face up on the trail, its left arm soaked in blood.

This *hombre* is plenty dead, Morello said to himself. That meant that the loose horse belonged to him. Not a good prize for a poor Mexican waddy but a prize worth taking.

But before he could make a move to rope the horse he heard a strange gurgling noise and it came from the figure lying on the ground. Next thing the man's eyes opened and he seemed to stare right at Morello in a pleading manner.

Now, despite the general temptations of life, Morello was a moral man. He was an orphan who had been brought up by the Jesuits and he had a concern for his immortal soul. So he got down from his horse and bent over the wounded man. Maybe he should take his confession before the man closed his eyes for the last time.

Then, instead of dying, the man raised his hand and said, 'Water! For God's sake give me water.'

'Water. Of course, you want water,' Morello said, reaching for his canteen. He had heard that giving a man with a wound in his chest water might hasten his end but he reasoned a drop of water might make him die happy anyway; so he raised the man's head and brought the canteen to his lips. And the man took a gulp and winced. Then instead of dying he levered himself up by his right arm. 'You want to help me, amigo, get me up on my feet and on to my horse. I've got to get back to Horse.'

Morello had no idea who Horse was but he understood that this poor *hombre* who looked like some kind of Indian needed his help.

'You not good for riding. You ride, you die,' he warned the wounded man.

'Get me into the shade,' the man pleaded.

'Sure. I get you.' With great care the Mexican dragged him out of the sun. 'You hurt bad,' he said, examining the bloody wound with great care. 'You need doctor man or you die.' Morello didn't know much about medical matters but he did know there was a doctor in Simm City. The question was, how could he get this wounded man to Simm City in time?

He examined the wound more closely and saw that it wasn't quite as bad as he had thought. It was right up on the left shoulder, close to the collar bone but possibly too high for the lung. Bones could be broken and possibly the slug was still in there close to the bone. It was difficult to tell.

Morello didn't know what to do.

The wounded man groaned and gritted his teeth. Then, after a moment, he opened his eyes. 'I'm Running Deer,' he muttered. 'And I need to get to Horse Soldier.'

'Horse Soldier?' said Morello. 'Who is this Horse Soldier? You need doctor man, not Horse Soldier.'

Running Deer ground his teeth. 'Get me on my horse, for God's sake. I'll just lie there on the horse's back and you take me to Simm City. Can you do that?'

'We will try,' Morello said. After all, Simm City was as good as any other place. He might meet someone who would offer him a job. Morello believed in fate, only he called it guidance.

Getting Running Deer on to his feet was mighty difficult and getting him on to his horse was even more so. But eventually he was in the saddle, leaning forward. Well, I made it, Running Deer said to himself. 'You get me to that bone setter in Simm City, I promise you a reward,' he said to Morello.

'I get you there, dead or alive,' Morello said.

They rode off gently towards the city.

*

57

After his meeting with Mingo in Simm City, Horse Soldier rode back to the ranch and found his friend Ed Potkin tending the beasts.

'Well hi there, Horse,' Ed greeted. 'So you're back. 'Bout time too. It's close to sundown. You must come up for a bit of supper. A man can't do much on an empty stomach. You know that?'

'Thank you kindly, Ed.'

'Where's that Indian buddy of yourn?' Ed enquired.

Horse Soldier had to admit he had no idea.

'Seemed a right friendly soul,' Ed said. 'Phoebe took a real shine to him. Thought he had a good, honest face. Hope he didn't get himself into any kind of trouble out there. Are you any closer to solving the problem of Sarah and Clemy's whereabouts?'

'I'm not sure,' Horse Soldier admitted. Then he told Ed about the meeting up on the bluff and how he had followed Mingo as far as Simm City.

'That's dang strange,' Ed said. 'So you parleyed with him too. I don't get this, Horse. What's the man playing at? And what's happening to you? You mean you didn't force him to take you to where Sarah and Clemy are being held?'

Horse Soldier didn't reply. Though he regarded Ed as a friend he couldn't let him in on his plans.

'By the way, Horse,' Ed said. 'A friend of mine dropped by earlier. Chuck Rivers. You might have met him one time. Says he knows you,'

Horse Soldier did remember Rivers, a man with a long nose who prided himself on knowing the gossip from all round the territory. 'Sure, I remember Rivers.'

'Sent his regards. Says he'd like to help you all he can.'

'That's real kind of him.' Horse Soldier had no great liking for Rivers. He was too much of a snoop but a man with a problem needs all the help he can get.

'Came up with an interesting piece of information,' Ed added.

Horse Soldier pricked up his ears. 'Is that so?'

'You remember that old guy Ross McMee, that cabin he built some few years back hoping to attract a woman to live with him?'

'Heard tell of it,' Horse Soldier admitted.

'Well, that old buddy of mine, Chuck Rivers, says he thinks it must be occupied again since he saw smoke rising from the chimney when he was riding close by a day or two ago.'

Though Chuck Rivers had a long gossipy nose and Horse Soldier thought he was like an old gossip talking nonsense to her friends at the well, on this occasion the information struck him like the sound of a bell: smoke was rising from the Ross McMee place. This might just be the clue he was looking for.

He was already strapping on his gunbelt and checking his Winchester.

'You think that's where they're holding Sarah and Clemy?' the old man asked him.

'I don't know, Ed, but there's only one way to find out, isn't there?'

'But it'll soon be plumb dark as hell,' Ed Potkin said.

'That's just the time for looking,' Horse Soldier said. The McMee cabin is no more than thirty miles west of here.'

Ed paused for just one moment. 'Want me to come with you, Horse?'

'I think you should stay right here. Phoebe might need you.'

'That doesn't figure, Horse, Phoebe can look after the spread. I'm old but I can still ride and I used to be a pretty good shot, and two guns are better than one by any man's reckoning. But first we must eat.'

CHAPTER FIVE

It was almost dark when Morello rode into Simm City with
Running Deer drooping forward on his horse. The first
thing they encountered was a bunch of rowdies who had
ridden in from a neighbouring ranch.

'What's with the *hombre* on the horse?' one of them
shouted. 'Can't he take his booze?'

'He take a bullet in his shoulder,' Morello explained.
'He fit to die, maybe dead already.'

At the word 'dead' Running Deer raised his head a little
and stared at the rowdies.

'He's not dead, just wounded bad,' the cowpuncher
said. 'We better get him to the sawbones, see what he can
do.'

'Sawbones Higgins is in the saloon drinking with the
sheriff,' a helpful gentleman informed them.

'Ain't you called Morello?' another of the cowpunchers
said.

'That's me, sure 'nough,' Morello agreed.

'Well, I'm Big Jim. We worked together down New
Mexico way that time,' the cowpuncher said. 'The year

61

they gunned down on the Kid, remember?'

'I remember good,' Morello responded.

While they were reminiscing, someone went into the bar to summon Sawbones Higgins who came out with Sheriff Stafford in tow. Doc Higgins was a thin man with drooping moustaches and side-whiskers who always wore a dark jacket and a bowler hat which had earned him the nickname Doctor Death, but many a man and woman in Simm City owed him their lives. So he was a generally respected citizen.

He stood on the sidewalk and looked up at the ailing man. 'Better get him along to my place,' he said quietly, 'and we'll see just what we can do.' He took the horse by the bridle and led it along to his office half a block away.

Sheriff Stafford was fidgeting about and looking uneasily into the gathering darkness. 'What happened here?' he enquired.

'I don't savvy,' Morello said unhelpfully. 'Someone shoot the man. I find him. Bring him here.'

Stafford was a little more dutiful than he appeared to be. So he followed on down the main drag to the doctor's office.

Morello was describing in some detail to his buddy Big Jim, who was indeed of modest size, just how he had come upon Running Deer lying half-dead close by his horse. 'By the grace of the Big *Hombre* up there in the sky,' he added. 'I find him.'

Doctor Sawbones Higgins took considerable care in getting Running Deer off his horse and into his surgery. In fact he spent some time examining the wound when they lifted Running Deer on to the sidewalk.

'Lay him there,' he said. 'Gently does it. Cover his legs

with a horse blanket. Keep him from taking chill in the night air.'

After a preliminary examination, he had them lift the patient into the house where he was carried through to the surgery and laid on a surgical couch.

'Yes, yes, just so,' the doctor muttered. 'I see the bullet is still in the shoulder. I'll have to give you a shot of whiskey and extract it. You just bite hard on this gag and it won't be too bad, son.'

It felt like hell to Running Deer and he almost bit right through the gag, though to everyone's astonishment he didn't utter a sound. When the operation was over he went right off into a deep sleep and knew no more until the first cry of the morning bird.

Ed Potkin could navigate his way to the McMee cabin even in the dark and, when the moon came peering over the hills, he and Horse Soldier were well on their way. In years gone by Ed had been a scout with the Texas Rangers and, though his eyesight was somewhat dimmer now, he still retained many of his old skills. In fact, guiding Horse Soldier through the night to the McMee place was something of an adventure to him.

Phoebe, his wife, was understandably concerned. She regarded Horse Soldier as something of a wild man and did not entirely approve of his occupation, though she liked him well enough.

'What do we aim to do?' Ed Potkin asked, as he and Horse Soldier rode along together.

'I don't exactly know,' Horse said. 'Just as long as we rescue Sarah and Clemy I don't care much but I want you to take care over this, Ed. I appreciate your help but I want you to come out of this in one piece. As far as I'm concerned, you're my guide and nothing more.'

'Well, we'll see about that,' the old man said. 'We'll have to just take things as they go.'

The ruined cabin wasn't so far away and Horse wondered at the foolishness of the kidnappers. How could these dumb clucks think that they could possibly avoid detection and in such an obvious place too? When they got close enough, Horse Soldier and Ed Potkin dismounted and went forward cautiously to the edge of a bluff. Horse lay down on his belly and handed Ed a bottle. 'Take a swing of that,' he said. 'Keep yourself good and warm.'

'Thank you, Horse, but I don't use it. It dulls the senses and I haven't got too much left so I aim to keep them as long as possible.'

Horse took that as good advice. He had often taken a swig or two when he was closing in on some killer; but now out of respect for Ed, he desisted.

Looking through his field glasses, he could see dim lights shining in the cabin and, just as the snooper had said, a spiral of smoke was rising from what was left of the stack.

'What do we aim to do?' Ed Potkin asked him.

'What I aim is to get in closer, see what I can find out,' Horse said. 'You stay and watch. I don't want for you to get yourself in too deep here.'

'I'm deep enough already,' Ed said. 'I want those two good creatures rescued too, you know.'

'Well, I appreciate that, but we've got be practical here. If anything gets rough that old Winchester of yours might come in handy.'

'Sure thing,' Ed agreed with some enthusiasm.

Horse Soldier crept forward and made his way stealthily towards the cabin. He knew there would be someone out there on lookout. The man would be sitting outside, probably nodding off to sleep and resentful at having to keep watch. 'Indians always attack at sunup and never at night,' he would be muttering to himself resentfully.

In fact the man sitting there was Spike Ovenwood and he was indeed cursing and taking swigs from a secret flask he carried. He figured there was nothing to worry about since, if anything happened, he could blast the hell out of any living creature that happened to approach too close to the cabin. In fact he had his Winchester propped up beside him and he had even thought of blasting off a round or two to keep the boys inside on their toes. Ovenwood felt somewhat disgruntled to be out there in the chill air when Vic Ridelle was playing somewhat discordantly on his harmonica. Ovenwood knew there would be dancing too! After all, hadn't he shot down that Indian, Running Deer? Nobody seemed to appreciate that, though it was the logical thing to do. One down and one to go, he thought.

He looked up into the old dead tree that dominated the near distance and imagined he could see a body swinging from it, to and fro, to and fro. That would be the struggling form of Horse Soldier choking out his last breath. Ovenwood had nothing personal against Horse Soldier, but Cal and Vic had promised a pot of gold to see that bounty hunter swing. So he would do his best.

What Ovenwood did not know was that Horse Soldier was right there behind the gnarled tree, crouching down low with his Winchester trained on him. He had crept up under cover of a ridge of cloud that covered the moon and now he was no more than twenty yards off, calculating his next move.

Horse Soldier peered out between some low branches and fixed his eyes on Ovenwood. He could even hear Ovenwood rambling on to himself about how he had tricked that skulking Indian and shot him dead. Though he was resentful, he was making the best of it and he even croaked out a few snatches of song to drown out the sound of the harmonica.

Godammit! Horse Soldier thought, someone's playing music in there. Like they were happy and having a good time! Anger boiled up in him so strongly that he was tempted to charge forward and blast off as many rounds at as many heads as he could. Bam! Bam! Bam! They'd all be writhing on the floor before they knew what was happening!

Only trouble was that Sarah and Clemy were in there and they might be killed in the scramble. Another thing, the door would be bolted anyway.

So Horse Soldier crouched down and considered his next move and it came quicker than he expected. Suddenly the door of the cabin creaked open and a form appeared. It was Daryl Fabre and he was laughing.

'Well now, buddy boy!' he crowed. 'Your turn to join in the dance. I've just stepped outside for a good wholesome breath of air.'

Horse Soldier could hear the harmonica wheezing away inside. And somebody was dancing! Would it be? Could it be Sarah?

Then Fabre spoke again. 'How's about you going in and joining the one, two, three step, Spike?'

'I'm no great tanglefoot waltzer,' Ovenwood declared. 'Who's dancing anyway?'

'Why, Mingo's dancing. He dances real good for a big man. A bit like a bear with two flannel feet.' Fabre gave a jeering laugh. 'He's waltzing around with that woman. She's no great dancer either. Stiff as a board. With a fine figure like that she should dance like a flowing river but . . . well, in the circumstances. . . .'

'In the circumstances she has to do as she's damned well told,' Ovenwood said. 'I might just go in there and take a turn or two. You never know what it might lead to, do you now?' It was clear from the sound of his voice that Ovenwood gave Fabre a broad wink.

The two men guffawed together crudely and Ovenwood disappeared into the cabin still laughing.

Fabre chuckled to himself and sat down on the bench. He placed his Winchester across his knees and seemed to consider the weather. The moon shone out from behind a shawl of cloud and lit up his grinning face. He was nodding with satisfaction and muttering to himself. 'That Mingo has his own ideas about womankind,' he said to himself.

He reached into his pocket and pulled out a tobacco pouch. Then he began to fill an old cob pipe. But, despite the pipe, Fabre wasn't a man to rest easy. So, after a second, he got up and started prowling restlessly to and fro. First he looked up at the gathering cloud and then he looked out right and left across the plain. After that he seemed to stare out towards the bluff where old Ed Potkin was waiting patiently for whatever might happen.

'Mingo has his own ideas about womankind.' The words echoed through Horse Soldier's head. And what might they be, he wondered? He was still consumed by the urge to rush towards the cabin, smash the windows and start shooting those inside. But once more he restrained himself.

As he crouched behind the gnarled trunk of the dead tree he saw Daryl Fabre move towards him as though drawn by some strange impulse. Fabre walked over to the tree and stared right up into the branches and laughed. 'That's where you'll dangle, buddy boy,' he said to himself. 'That's where you'll be swinging like a rotten fruit.' He leaned on the dead trunk and sniggered.

Horse Soldier had risen and pressed himself close against the trunk as Fabre moved across smoking his pipe. Now they were only a couple of feet apart, so close that Horse Soldier could have reached out and touched him.

Fabre was still sniggering to himself as he turned and suddenly saw the face of Horse Soldier staring at him from behind a lower branch. He drew back with a gasp, but was too late. Horse Soldier brought the barrel of his Winchester down as hard as he could on his head. There was a dull pulpy sound; an expression of shocked amazement appeared on the sniggering man's face as he jerked back and slid down the trunk and on to the ground. His newly lit pipe bounced a couple of times and lay, smouldering still.

Horse looked down at the twitching body and saw the blood spreading across its temple. Without looking closer, he could see that Daryl Fabre was as dead as though he had never been born. So he stepped over the body without regret and moved towards the cabin.

He knew the door was locked but part of the window was clear. He could hear the noise of the harmonica and he looked in sideways to avoid being detected. He couldn't see Vic Ridelle playing his harmonica but he saw the forms of two people shuffling together in a kind of macabre dance movement. One was a man and the other was a woman. The man danced like a bear and the woman hung like a rag doll in his arms.

The man was Mingo and the woman was Horse Soldier's wife, Sarah.

Ed Potkin was lying stretched out surveying the scene through field glasses from the bluff. He was deeply apprehensive yet excited. The whole thing reminded him of his days as a guide in the Texas Rangers but he wondered what the hell Horse Soldier was doing down there. He knew that Horse would stop at nothing to free his wife and daughter from those critters from hell, but he worried they might all end up dead.

The glasses had quite good magnification but Ed couldn't see as much as he wanted to and what he did see worried him more than somewhat. He saw light flickering in the windows of the cabin and men coming and going. He even saw the flare of Daryl Fabre's pipe as he lit it.

Dang fool! he thought. A little bit closer and I could have snuffed it out and him too with it. And then, as if by some kind of thought fulfilment process he saw Fabre buckle and fall to the ground. There was no sound of gunfire or any other indication. The man just dropped and lay still. Just by that old dead tree, too! Ed had a mighty strong suspicion of dead trees. Like they spread a kind of spell on the *hombres* who stood too close to them.

Like standing close to a tree when there was lightning around.

Then he saw the shadow of a man move close to the window and peer inside. That's Horse, he thought. What the hell does he aim to do now?

And then after a moment Horse disappeared.

Ed Potkin waited and waited but the night rolled on and nothing more happened until the door of the cabin was flung open and another man emerged. He seemed to look about for several seconds before he saw the body of the dead man lying on the ground. After that all hell broke loose. Men spilled out of the cabin and there was so much hollering and shouting that Ed could almost have laughed if the situation hadn't been so serious.

After that things became ominously quiet again.

Ed was half drowsing when Horse Soldier slid down beside him.

'What in tarnation is happening down there?' Ed asked him.

'What happened is I killed a man and there was stomping in the shack,' Horse Soldier explained.

Ed knew about the killing. 'They deserve it, the whole bunch of them,' he said. But he was surprised about the dancing. 'Sarah wouldn't dance with those hellrakers,' he said. 'Not willingly, that is. What are we going to do, Horse?'

Horse Soldier was perplexed. 'One thing's for sure, I have to stay here and watch for the right moment,' he said without too much conviction.

'And I must stay and watch with you, Horse. Phoebe can manage right well without me. I sometimes wonder just exactly what my role is, anyway.' He gave a grim chuckle.

'But one thing I should do: if you're set on staying here, I'm going back to provision us up. If we're going to play our hand with good sense, we need good provender. If I ride back to the spread, I can be back by sunup. How would that be?'

Horse Soldier had to admit that that would be fine. At least it would keep the old man out of trouble till morning.

In the cabin panic had broken loose. The dancing had come to an end and, much to her relief, Sarah had been pushed back into the other room where Clemy had fallen into an exhausted sleep. Now Mingo was guarding them again.

The wall between the two rooms was not quite paper thin but it was thin enough to allow Sarah to hear most of what was being said, if only that brute Mingo would stop talking.

Now Gus Daniel was holding forth. 'I told you it was a mistake, Cal, didn't I, taking a place like this? We're just like sitting ducks in here.'

'Yeah, he has a point,' Ridelle agreed. 'That Horse Soldier knows all the tricks in the trade and a few more beside. He must have snuck right up to kill Fabre like he did. Fabre didn't have time to take more than three puffs on his pipe before he was killed.'

'Well, maybe he died happy, eh?' Cal Livermore joked.

'Happy or unhappy, he died,' Gus Daniel said. 'That's the main consideration. We should have ridden right up to Horse Soldier's door and shot down his kin in front of him and then strung him up. That would have been better than prancing around in this stinking hole.'

71

'What do you suggest?' Cal Livermore asked him.

At that moment Sarah might have learned something but Mingo's voice drowned out the other speakers. 'Did you enjoy the dance, pretty woman?' he asked.

'I wasn't dancing,' she declared. 'I was just being hauled around by you.'

Mingo chuckled. 'That's not the right tone to adopt,' he said, 'especially in view of I might be your saviour.'

Sarah heard the words and noted the shifting timbre of Mingo's voice. Could it be that this gorilla of a man was trying to make some kind of proposal to her, a proposal that might actually save her and Clemy? 'What kind of saviour would you be?' she asked.

'Any kind of saviour you might want,' the big man said. 'I'm not saying I can read your old man's mind but I believe he might want you alive better than dead.'

Be cautious here, a voice said in a dark corner of Sarah's head. This gorilla of a man has some hidden purpose.

'What are you saying to me?' she asked him directly.

Mingo was staring at her, if not with admiration, at least with appreciation. 'I don't want you dead. We could do a deal if you play your cards right.'

'How would I do that?' she asked him.

'Well, just let me lay it out for you,' he said.

Come sun-up in Simm City the cocks were crowing and Running Deer was just opening his eyes. What he saw was a man in a dark suit who looked like an undertaker. In fact it flashed across Running Deer's mind that it was the Devil himself come to carry him off to Hell. Except that the supposed devil was taking his pulse and sounding his chest.

'Remarkable,' the doctor said. 'You have a very strong constitution, my man, and I think you'll last as long as it takes before you get another bullet in your chest a little further down. Do you feel hungry?'

Running Deer felt as hungry as hell and his left shoulder was as stiff and aching like hell, too!

'Thank you, Doc,' he said. 'When will it be OK to pull out of here?'

'Well, if you want that wound to heal properly you should rest up for at least a week and longer, if possible.'

'Well, that's going to be a mite inconvenient in view of the fact I have obligations to fulfil.'

'Well, if those obligations involve toting a gun I suggest you push them aside for the moment. That is if you want to live to tell the tale.'

The doctor might have a said more, but at that moment his wife opened the door to admit a visitor. It was Morello. He looked across at Running Dear and said. 'I come to see the wounded fellow. He doing well, Señor Sawbones?'

Doctor Higgins ignored the put down but he wasn't too happy about the way Morello had invaded his surgery. 'This man needs rest. He's lost a deal of blood.' His moustache quivered as he spoke.

'That's OK,' Morello said. 'You heard tell of the Good Samaritan, Doc? Well that guy is Morello. I come to make sure the man I rescue from the death jaw is rising from the stone dead.'

Despite his reputation, Dr Higgins wasn't without a sense of humour. 'Well,' he smiled behind his moustaches, 'I'll give you three minutes to talk to the man left for dead on the wayside and then you must vamoose. You understand?'

Morello nodded his head vigorously. 'Me *sabe* plenty, Señor Curandero.'

But Doc Higgins was even more surprised when Morello was followed into the surgery by two more men. One was Big Jim and the other was the doctor's drinking buddy, Sheriff Stafford.

Big Jim shuffled up behind Morello and listened intently as Morello spoke to Running Deer. 'I think you have miracle here,' he said. 'I take you for dead and now you rise up again.'

Running Deer winced. 'Well, my good friend, I have to thank you for that miracle and now I have to get back into my saddle and ride back to my partner Horse Soldier because we have a deal together.'

'What kind of deal is that?' Sheriff Stafford asked. Though he often appeared to be dozing in his rocking-chair he took in a good deal more than he appeared to. He remembered the somewhat menacing Horse Soldier well and he knew that Sarah his wife and his daughter Clemy had gone missing. He remembered seeing the stranger Running Deer and that Horse Soldier had met him in Stan Balding's saloon. He also remembered that later Horse Soldier had met a big bear of a man and how they had drunk beer together and afterwards had gone outside to sit together on the sidewalk deep in conversation. From Sheriff Stafford's point of view it was all very odd and suspicious!

While Morello was talking to Running Deer, Stafford was conferring with Doc Higgins. 'I think I'd like to ask your patient one or two questions,' he said.

'Well, I guess you can,' the doctor conceded, 'if it doesn't take too long. I don't want another patient dying on my hands, do I?'

Sheriff Stafford went over to the sickbed and ordered the others out of the room. Then he sat down on a stool. 'Listen,' he said, 'as Sheriff of Simm City I have to ask you a few questions. I want to hear what you know about Horse Soldier and this kidnapping. If anything happens in this town it's my responsibility to look into it.' While he was talking his eyes were darting every whichway, first to the sickbed and then on the ceiling, but he never looked directly into Running Deer's eyes.

'OK, Sheriff,' Running Deer said and he spilled out all he knew about the kidnapping, including the truth about Mingo and Spike Ovenwood, the man he had been trailing. Running Deer considered himself to be an expert tracker, so he was reluctant to admit that Ovenwood had led him to a place where he could gun down on him easily and Sheriff Stafford was discreet enough to avoid emphasizing the point.

'So that's how you got yourself shot,' he ruminated. Stafford's mind went back to the meeting between Horse Soldier and the big man in the saloon. 'Mighty strange that Horse Soldier should be having a drink with one of the kidnappers,' he said aloud.

Running Deer opened his eyes real wide: it was the first he had heard of the meeting. And it was the first Sheriff Stafford had heard about Mingo being one of the gang. 'Sounds like that Mingo guy is playing a very close game,' he said.

Running Deer went very quiet for a moment. He was turning the whole situation over in his mind. 'Listen, Sheriff,' he said, 'I need to get into the saddle as quick as I can. Horse Soldier is going to need all the help he can get to smoke out those killers.'

'Except you don't know where they are holed up, do you?' the sheriff replied. He was indeed a cautious man who hated to wade in out of his depth.

'Sheriff, why don't you ride over to the Potkin place and make enquires? Ed Potkin and his wife are good friends to Horse's family and Ed might know something.'

'Well, I guess I could do that,' Sheriff Stafford agreed. After all, making a few enquiries didn't amount to much, did it?

CHAPTER SIX

Horse Soldier had been lying there on the bluff most of the night. There was a little pool up there where his horse could drink and there was enough rough pasture for it to graze. But Horse wasn't thinking about food: he was worried sick about Sarah and Clemy and he couldn't get the picture of Sarah dancing with that gorilla Mingo out of his mind. Even so he dropped off into an uneasy sleep once or twice. The first time, he woke with a start and saw that the cabin lay like a sleeping ghost in the valley. Maybe I should creep down there and blast my way in while they're snoring and rescue Sarah and Clemy, but that's taking too much of a chance. If either Sarah or Clemy died I would never stop blaming myself!

Then, well on in the night towards sun-up, he started up again and saw something stirring down there. Dark figures were moving among the horses in the ramshackle barn. There was no light, just those obscure figures flitting about in the darkness.

The next instant, Ed Potkin crept in beside him. 'I brought the rations, enough for a week if needs be and extra feed for the horses,' he said quietly. Though Ed's knees creaked somewhat, he was still surprisingly nimble. Then he sat up quickly and squinted down at the cabin through glasses. 'Jumping Jehosephat, what's going on down there?'

Horse Soldier was peering through his glasses too, and now he saw the ghostly figures mounting up and one or two circling round. 'They're pulling out!' he said. 'They're riding off somewhere.'

'You're damned right they are!" Ed exclaimed. 'And I do believe I can see Sarah and Clemy among them.'

Horse quickly identified Sarah but he couldn't at first make out Clemy. 'I don't see Clemy,' he said and his heart was thumping under his ribs. Then he saw her. She was mounted in front of one of the men and she was struggling in vain to free herself.

'That kid has got grit,' Ed said in admiration as he saw her too.

'Keep yourself damned still!' Gus Daniel muttered angrily. That's if you want to live to see this day through!' Gus Daniel had no love for children. He didn't love anybody. That was part of his trouble.

'Where are you taking us?' Clemy demanded.

Sarah was close by on another horse. She had her hands tied together in front of her and her horse was being led by Vic Ridelle. Mingo was riding close keeping an eye on her.

Sarah half turned in her saddle and said. 'Keep still, Clemy. We both have to do as we're bid.'

'That's the truth, ma'am,' Mingo agreed. 'Surely everything's going to be all right, girl, as long as you do as we tell you.'

Clemy thrust out her lip and began to think. Most of the night she had been only half asleep and towards morning she had heard their kidnappers arguing among themselves.

'The best thing we can do is to light out from here,' Cal Livermore had said. 'I never liked the idea of holing up here in the first place. That Horse Soldier is as tricky as a whole bunch of coyotes.'

'Well, you're right about that,' Gus Daniel had agreed. The picture of Daryl Fabre's staring corpse lying by the gnarled tree hadn't appealed to him one little bit.

Vic Ridelle had made no further objection. So it was agreed that just before sun-up they would ride out into the darkness and make their escape. They had only one final trick up their sleeves and that was down to Spike Ovenwood and Charlie Springfield.

Horse Soldier and Ed Potkin were just about to mount up when something surprising happened. The whole cabin suddenly exploded in a burst of flame.

'What the hell!' Ed said. 'What are those madmen doing now, for Gawd's sake?'

In a moment of panic Horse Soldier thought Sarah and Clemy were being sacrificed to the flames. Before he had time to think, he had mounted his horse and was ready to gallop down towards the flaming cabin.

'Wait!' shouted Ed. 'Maybe that's what they want!' He gathered up the supplies, stowed them in his saddle-bag and mounted up.

Together they rode down towards the cabin. As they drew closer and the flames lit them up someone fired off

two shots in quick succession. One of them flew danger-
ously close to Horse Soldier's head. The other grazed Ed
in the leg and struck his horse in the belly. The horse
reared up and fell, pinning Ed to the ground.

Horse Soldier swung his horse round and dismounted.
Ed's horse was rolling in agony and kicking out its legs and
Ed was crying out too. Fortunately for Ed the horse rolled
away from him and tried to get on to its feet. Then
another shot hit the creature full in the head and it
dropped down like a stone.

Horse Soldier bent over Ed to see how badly he had
been hit. The old-timer dragged himself away from the
dead horse and tried to get on to his knees. Then he gave
a cry and flopped down. 'I been hit!' he said.

'Lie still,' Horse Soldier said. 'Lie still while I take a
look see.' He examined the injured leg and found that the
bullet had grazed it just below the knee before striking the
horse's side. But he was more concerned about the left leg
where the horse had rolled on to Ed.

'I think your left leg is broken,' Horse said. 'We need to
patch you up and stop the bleeding and then get you to
the doc.'

'What the hell d'you do that for?' Cal Livermore asked
Spike Ovenwood as the whole bunch rode away.

'Seemed a good idea,' Spike Ovenwood said. 'I think I
hit the old man and I nearly winged Horse Soldier too.
With the old man hit Horse Soldier won't rightly know
what to do.'

Charlie Springfield wasn't so happy. 'You damned kill
Horse Soldier, what's the good of that?'

'I didn't aim to kill Horse Soldier,' Ovenwood said. 'If I

aim to kill a man he usually drops down and stays down.'

The others didn't argue with that though both Cal Livermore and Vic Ridelle were beginning to think Ovenwood was more of a liability than an asset. An *hombre* who boasts about being good with a gun can land you in a whole lot of trouble!

It was very dark and the moon hadn't yet risen. So Clemy could scarcely see her mother jogging along ahead of her. Clemy was listening out to hear whether her father was riding close behind them. Maybe he would track in close and rope Mingo from the horse and drag him down to the ground. Clemy knew that was mere fantasy. So she started thinking and praying that they would all be safe. Sometime before the sun got up the whole party would need to stop and that would be her chance. She was beginning to think these kidnappers were not as smart as they thought they were and the fact that they meant to kill her father made her more determined than ever to do something to thwart them. So she kept herself still and tried to work out a plan.

Come sun-up Phoebe Potkin was out in the yard. She was dealing with her chores as usual and she was about to ride down to Sarah Millar's place to tend to things there. Phoebe was worried. She was concerned about Sarah and Clemy and she was worried about her man Ed, who, as she would have said, was '*no spring chicken*', though she knew he was a tough old rooster who was willing to bite off a lot more than he could chew. When, during the night, he had dropped in to pick up rations for as long as a week she wondered whether he had gone slightly crazy! And that was partly down to Horse Soldier who was, in her opinion, also somewhat loco and not a particularly good husband and father either.

Phoebe was complaining bitterly to her herself when she saw three riders coming towards her from the direction of Simm City. Two of them she didn't recognize but the third was Sheriff Stafford, and this was alarming since Sheriff Stafford seldom left Simm City. Indeed he had the reputation for the being the laziest sheriff that Simm City had ever had.

When they drew close Sheriff Stafford touched his Stetson and greeted her. 'Morning, Mrs Potkin,' he intoned. 'Is your man about? I'd favour a word with him.'

She looked at the other two *hombres* and could recall having seen neither of them before. One of them was obviously Latino and the other was of modest size. The Latino was, indeed, Morello and smaller man was Big Jim.

Morello prided himself on his courtesy. So he lifted his hat right off his head and took a bow from his horse's back. 'It is pleasure we meet, Señora Potkin,' he said.

Phoebe was somewhat alarmed. When men spoke to her with such elaborate courtesy she wondered what might be in the air.

'Ed is away from home,' she explained to the sheriff. 'He left early. I believe he's heading for that ruined cabin old man McMee built some years back. It's about thirty miles from here.'

Sheriff Stafford nodded grimly and focused his eyes briefly on Phoebe. 'Now, why would he do that, Mrs Potkin?'

Phoebe looked at Morello and he smiled encouragement at her.

'That's because Horse Soldier thinks they're holding

Sarah and Clemy there,' she said. 'Horse and that half-Indian man, Running Deer McVicar, are trying to free Sarah and Clemy. I don't know where Running Deer is at the moment. I haven't seen him for a day or two.'

'That because Running Deer get himself shot,' Morello explained.

Sheriff Stafford gave Morello a sharp look and said, 'No need to alarm yourself, Mrs Potkin. Running Deer is in the care of Dr Higgins right now and we aim to ride right up to that McMee place and sort the whole thing out before there's any more gunplay.'

Phoebe nodded in agreement. 'I do hope you're right on that, Sheriff. And when you see my husband, tell him to come back here as fast as he can. He's too old to be riding around and shooting at people. Ed's just too old.'

Sheriff Stafford touched his hat again. 'I'll be sure to tell him that, Mrs Potkin.'

Morello took off his hat and made an elaborate bow again. 'We do everything, Señora Potkin. You do not worry none.'

Big Jim said nothing.

The three men turned their horses and rode off in the direction of the McMee cabin.

The sun was right up now and Horse Soldier was still attending to Ed Potkin's broken leg. Ed was gritting his teeth and shivering. 'If only I had had the sense to bring us a spare horse you could have got me into the saddle and we could have ridden on after those pizonous snakes and rescued Sarah and Clemy.'

If only it had been as easy as that! Horse thought. He was wondering what he could do next when he looked up and saw the three riders cantering towards them. At first he thought the kidnappers had sent out men to kill them, but, as they drew closer, he recognized Sheriff Stafford.

The sheriff rode right up and looked down at Ed Potkin. 'You hurt bad, Ed?' he said.

'Left leg seems to be broke,' Ed said. 'Other than that, a slug grazed my right leg and killed my hoss.'

Stafford and the other two looked towards the McMee cabin which was still blazing as if a thunderbolt had struck it 'What happened? You smoke them out?' the sheriff asked.

Horse told the sheriff what had happened.

'So, did you see Sarah and young Clemy?' Stafford asked.

'I saw them,' Horse said bitterly. He didn't go into details but mentioned that the kidnappers had set the cabin alight and had ridden off, taking Sarah and Clemy with them.

'So what do you aim to do?' the sheriff asked.

'I'm going to ride right after them,' Horse said grimly. 'Only thing I can do.'

Stafford looked doubtfully at the wounded man. 'We got to get Ed back to Doc Higgins pronto,' he said.

'*Sí, sí,*' Morello agreed.

Horse Soldier had already managed to apply a primitive dressing on to the wound which didn't seem to be much more than a graze. Now they managed to get a splint on the broken leg and together they hoisted Ed on to one of the horses.

'I guess it's my responsibility to take Ed back to the doc,' the sheriff said. 'What you do now, Horse, is down to you.'

'Well, I can ride alone,' Horse said. 'I usually do, anyway.'

'I ride with you,' Morello suddenly piped up. 'We make free your woman and girl. I mucho good tracker and I shoot good too. I come with you.'

Horse wasn't sure about that. After all he didn't know anything about this stranger who talked in such a queer lingo. Nevertheless, Morello had saved Running Deer, so he must have some good qualities. Ed was on Big Jim's horse and Big Jim could mount up behind him. It was clear that Sheriff Stafford had no taste for riding on out of his territory and tangling with the kidnappers.

'OK,' Horse Soldier said, 'so we continue.'

After the sheriff and Big Jim had started back towards Simm City, Horse and Morello went down to the blazing cabin. Horse didn't know what to say to Morello but Morello did most of the talking anyway.

'This not good thing, Mr Horse,' he said. 'We follow the tracks and soon catch up on those not-so-good *hombres*. They not let your woman go, we kill them good.'

'I'll kill them sure enough,' Horse said. 'But Sarah and Clemy have to be saved. That's the only thing that matters.'

'*Sí, sí*,' Morello agreed eagerly. 'How many we have to kill?'

'Six, I figure,' Horse said. He wasn't sure about the number. He was still thinking about his meeting with Mingo and the agreement they had reached. 'What's in this for you, anyway?' he asked the Mexican.

Morello had dismounted and he was studying the tracks and the horse droppings. 'What's in it for me is I go for

85

Running Deer. He very brave but stupid getting himself shot like that.'

'You some kind of good Samaritan like it says in the Good Book?' Horse Soldier said.

'*Sí, sí*, sure!' Morello beamed. 'I learned that from Jesuit teachers. I have big hate for men who do bad things like that.' He pointed where the tracks led. 'We follow now. They not so far ahead.'

'Well, don't do anything unless I tell you, that's all.'

'OK, we work together.'

Horse wasn't happy. He was thinking what a pity it was that Running Deer had been hit. Running Deer had been a man you could rely on. As for this man, was he all mouth?

Thus they rode on quite briskly, following the tracks.

Charlie Springfield was beginning to wonder what he had got himself into. All he could hear was Spike Ovenwood boasting about how easily he could have killed Horse Soldier, just like a duck paddling in a creek, and Gus Daniel continually growled at him to 'shut that great hole you call a mouth'. Cal Livermore had offered Charlie a big reward if he would ride with them to silence that bounty hunter who had wrought so much damage throughout the territory. Now Charlie was beginning to think he had been duped. He was thinking of Daryl Fabre too. Finding him out there stone cold dead under the withered old tree had been kind of creepy as though some phantom had crawled up through the cold night air and struck him down, just as he was sucking on his pipe too! It was downright eerie! So, as Charlie rode along with the others, he kept a wary eye out, looking every whichway across the undulating plain.

Clemy was looking out in every direction too. Although she wasn't tied, she was held firmly in Mingo's bear-like grasp.

'Don't you fret, missy,' Mingo whispered to calm her. 'Everything's going to be all right.'

Clemy tossed her head. 'Where are we going?' she asked for the umpteenth time.

The truth was that Mingo had no idea where they were headed, or how long it would take. He figured Cal Livermore had that all worked out.

As they rode on, although it was hot and muggy, big clouds had started to gather over the distant hills to the west and a veil of rain came drifting towards them. 'There's a storm coming in,' Vic Ridelle said. 'Maybe we should stop and rest up by that bunch of trees over there.'

'Nobody stops by trees in a storm,' Gus Daniel retorted, 'not unless you want to be struck down by lightning.'

'A buddy of mine was struck by lightning once,' Spike Ovenwood said helpfully. 'I was just riding up to join him when he lit up like a damned Christmas tree and just burned away like a Roman candle.'

'Maybe we should ride up to those rocks up there,' Gus Daniel suggested. 'They should give us some shelter, at least for a while. I want to take a leak, anyway.'

The rock formation was much more substantial than it looked from a distance. The Indians had named it Scrambling Rocks. The party reached it just before the storm swept over the prairie. And that was some storm, with great cannonades of thunder and vivid flashes of lightning. The horses started bucking and rearing and whinnying in terror, and the men dismounted and took refuge in whatever crevices and caves they could find.

Mingo had to release Clemy and Sarah and she took refuge in a narrow crevice just in time. Cal Livermore and Vic Ridelle ordered that the horses should be hobbled which was no easy task since the horses were lashing out in panic in all directions.

'A man could get himself killed doing this!' Spike Ovenwood complained to the wind.

Mingo was too big to squeeze into any of the crevices. So he took shelter under a crooked little tree. If the lightning wanted to get him, then so be it! Ridelle and Livermore, Daniel, Springfield, and Ovenwood all managed to find spaces they could cram themselves into.

There was a vivid flash of lightning that seemed to splash right against the tree where Mingo was sheltering but he had ducked back behind a huge rock, just in time. My Gawd! he thought, is this the Lord's judgement on me?

Clemy was crammed in next to her mother; Sarah still had her wrists lashed together with rawhide.

'Be brave,' Sarah said to Clemy above the raging wind. 'Please don't do anything stupid. These men wouldn't think twice about killing you.'

'They want to get my daddy,' Clemy said. 'I heard them talking in the night. But we can't let them do that, can we?'

Sarah didn't know what to say. She had tried to think of what to do so hard that she felt nauseous. Then she noticed that the horse that Spike Ovenwood had been riding hadn't been properly hobbled. Its reins had been looped loosely over a rock. Clemy, who had been riding since before she could walk, had noticed it too.

'Mummy,' she said, 'I've got to do something to help. I'm going to make a break out of here and find Daddy.'

Sarah was shivering, partly from the cold and partly from fear. 'Please don't do that, Clemy. These men will shoot you if you do!'

Clemy said nothing. She peeped out and saw Mingo crouching a metre away with his hat pulled down over his eyes. From where they were hiding she couldn't see anybody else. Clemy had a lot of her father in her. She crouched there, calculating her chances. Storms don't last for ever and they tend to pulse over the prairie in waves. When the next wave subsided, that would be her best chance. So she squeezed her mother's arm and coiled like a spring to get herself ready.

The rain died suddenly as quickly as it had come and she made her move. She darted out quickly and grabbed the horse's reins. She jerked them from the rock that held them and leaped on to its back. The horse bucked in panic and tried to shake her off. But Clemy was a true farm girl and she clung on like a leech. In a fraction of a second she was in the saddle, digging her heels into the horse's side.

'What in hell's name!' It was Spike Ovenwood bellowing out. He lumbered out from his hole in the rocks and tried to make a grab for the prancing horse. The horse lashed out with its hoof and caught him right on the shoulder. He fell back against Charlie Springfield who was fumbling for his shooter.

'Shoot!' Spike Ovenwood shouted. 'Shoot that damned kid!'

'Please don't shoot!' Sarah pleaded.

'Shoot the bitch!' Vic Ridelle bellowed.

Charlie Springfield fired a shot at the rapidly retreating figure, but the next instant the huge bulk of Mingo had fallen across him and knocked the Colt clean out of his hand.

Now Vic Ridelle was out in the open and he fired off a couple of rounds in quick succession. 'Damn it!' he raged, as Clemy and the horse were swallowed up by the rain.

Sarah was screaming and the rain came down again like steel rods.

Horse Soldier and Morello were out in the open when they saw the storm trailing in across the plain. Horse made a quick decision. He checked the direction of the tracks and turned his horse towards a stand of trees.

'What we do?' Morello said.

'We take shelter and put on our capes,' Horse Soldier said.

They made for a little bluff with a fringe of trees.

'OK,' Morello said. 'What we do now?'

'We wait,' Horse Soldier said. 'We sit out the storm and wait.' He had suddenly become grimly calm. He knew that the kidnappers were about to be caught too and they would have to take shelter where they could. He figured that the kidnappers wouldn't know the country as well as he knew it.

When he and Morello reached the sheltering place he reached into his saddle-bag and produced a couple of capes. He handed one to Morello and donned the other himself. Then he reached into his saddle-bag again and produced another cape which he threw over his horse's back.

'You keep horse dry!' Morello marvelled.

'Always look after your horse,' Horse said. 'You look after your beast he won't let you down.'

Morello stared at him in amazement; he had never looked at it in that way before. So he led his horse into the most sheltered place he could find and tethered it to a small pine.

'We'll be OK in here,' Horse Soldier told him. 'If the lightning strikes it will more than likely hit one of those trees higher up.'

When the storm rode in over the bluff they were comparatively sheltered but, as Horse had predicted, one of the trees further up was struck by lightning and it keeled right over and slid down into an arroyo.

'Plenty water,' Morello observed, and he was right: already rainwater was gushing into the arroyo from further up the bluff.

Then, as the storm subsided, they both heard the shots. One, two, three, Horse counted. What was happening out there? Were those killers executing Sarah and Clemy, or were they shooting at one another?

'They shooting at something,' Morello declared somewhat irrelevantly. Horse reasoned that the kidnappers were in some kind of panic and that he must ride on as quickly as he could.

As soon as the storm rolled on across the prairie towards Simm City he and Morello mounted up and rode out in the direction from where the shots had come. Horse had a pretty good idea where the kidnappers had taken shelter and he wanted to catch up with them pronto.

*

91

Back in Simm City, Doc Higgins was examining Ed Potkin's wound. Running Deer was hopping about, holding on to chairs to keep his balance. The wound in his shoulder was still aching and throbbing but he was raring to go.

'Listen, Doc,' he said. 'I'm grateful for all you've done, but now it's time to get out of here. I've got an appointment with those poisonous killers who shot my father and Horse will be expecting me.'

'Like I told you, you're in no position to ride anywhere,' Doctor Higgins reminded him. 'Look what happened to Ed here. He's in no position to ride either. Horse Soldier has to look after himself.'

'That's as maybe,' Ed Potkin said. 'But we must do something to help before Sarah and the girl get hurt.' He turned pointedly to Sheriff Stafford who was standing by the door. 'This is a matter for the law, ain't it, Sheriff?'

Sheriff Stafford was biting his lip and blinking his eyes and may have been wondering why he had accepted the sheriff's badge. It was beginning to look as though he ought to do something to justify his position.

'And someone needs to ride and tell Phoebe I'm still alive,' Ed Potkin put in. 'If I can't ride out and help Horse at least I can get myself home.'

'Well, we'll get you on to the buckboard,' Doc Higgins said. 'And I'll drive you home.'

At that moment Big Jim stuck his head in through the doorway. 'Tell you what I'll do,' he said. 'You can all rest easy. I'll ride out to that cabin and I'll go look for my old buddy, Morello. Morello and Horse Soldier could do with another gun. That is if I can find them.'

'They could be anywhere,' Ed said pessimistically. 'Like

looking for a needle in a haystack.'

Big Jim was about to retort that he was a good tracker and could follow anything that had moved through the land when the storm struck Simm City.

After the storm abated Horse Soldier and Morello got their things together and rode on.

'I have a hunch where those no-good killers are,' he muttered to himself.

'You know where they headed?' Morello said.

Morello was beginning to irritate Horse who had had more than enough of his jabber. Horse wanted to concentrate on his next move though he had no idea what to do next. The shots floating in on the breeze had done nothing to calm his nerves. Anything could have happened out there.

'Look!' Morello said suddenly, pointing away to the left.

Another distraction, Horse Soldier thought, but then he turned and saw the horse way off in the distance. It looked like a stampeding mustang that had broken free. Then, when he brought his binoculars to his eye, he saw there was a rider and he or she was very small, riding close to the horse's shoulder.

'Great God!' he said, 'that looks like Clemy!'

'Clemy, your *muchacha*?' Morello asked.

Horse was still trying to focus the binoculars. 'That's Clemy all right!' he said. The girl on the horse was so far off he knew that they hadn't a hope of catching up with her. Where would she go? Was one of those low-down skunks following her, trying to gun her down.

He spurred his mount and started at a gallop, and Morello followed after him quickly. Soon he and Horse were riding stirrup to stirrup.

'Why not we fire a shot?' Morello suggested breathlessly. 'Attract attention!'

That was a good idea, except that Clemy might think it was one of the kidnappers riding in pursuit. And then Morello took off his sombrero and started waving it and hollering, a gesture most killers wouldn't have thought of. Horse knew Clemy would never hear that voice; so drew his Colt and fired a shot into the air.

He saw Clemy turn in the saddle. The next moment she had reined in her mount and turned towards them.

'The *muchacha* see us!' Morello cried, still waving his sombrero furiously.

For a moment Clemy didn't know whether to gallop on or ride towards the two men. She saw that one was waving a Mexican sombrero and the other had his arm held high. She screwed up her eyes and peered towards them and then something about the way Horse Soldier moved reassured her and she knew it was her father. She had ridden her horse hell for leather away from the kidnappers and he was blown. So she trailed the reins and let it recover. As the two riders cantered closer she knew she was right.

Horse Soldier rode right up to her and lifted her out of the saddle.

'Daddy!' she said. 'It's you! I thought you would come.'

Horse Soldier was amazed at how much she had grown up since he had last seen her. She was now sobbing her heart out against him.

'So you broke free!' he said in astonishment.

'They've still got Mummy!' she said. 'We have to rescue her.'

'We rescue, don't you worry,' Morello said.

Then the full story came rushing out and Clemy told her father everything, how cruel the kidnappers were, how her mother had her arms tied by the wrists, how they were always shouting at her and threatening to kill her.

'We've got to rescue her, Daddy! We've got to rescue her!' she pleaded.

'That's what we're gonna do, sweetheart,' Horse Soldier assured her.

CHAPTER SEVEN

After the storm had rolled away the kidnappers were in a state of some confusion. Spike Ovenwood's boastful confidence had been particularly shaken since he had lost his horse and to a mere chit of a girl.

'I could have shot that kid right down,' he complained, 'if you hadn't knocked yourself against my arm, Mingo. Why did you do that?'

Mingo offered no excuse. 'Just been nearly struck by lightning,' he said. 'Anyway, Ovenwood, you didn't tether your horse properly. So it was your fault the kid got away.'

Sarah had stopped screaming and become strangely silent. Of course, she was glad that Clemy had broken away, but had she been hit by one of those shots, she wondered, and might she be lying out there drenched to the skin and bleeding to death?

Now the storm had raged on, the sun had looked out bright and cheerful over the plain, and Sarah saw no sign of Clemy or the horse. She knew that Clemy could ride as well or better than most people, so she felt a slow tide of optimism rising in her heart. What happens now, she wondered? Where will these desperate men take me?

'My wrists are chaffing,' she said to Gus Daniel. 'Won't you please loosen these cruel ropes?'

Gus Daniel grinned and shook his head. 'Can't do that, lady. There's too much at stake here.'

Tod Ridelle then intervened. 'Want my opinion, you encouraged that kid to escape and that was a plumb foolish thing to do. She won't get far and even if she does it won't help you much. It just means we've got to keep an extra watch on you, that's all.'

But Sarah was listening to a dispute between Cal Livermore and Charlie Springfield who seemed to be the most disgruntled one of the bunch.

'We left that cabin and burned it down, now we're here, Cal. What do we aim to do next? That's what I want to know.'

'We can't lead that ornery critter right into New Mexico territory, can we? Stands to reason,' Cal Livermore said with a sneer.

'Well then, what's your conclusion?' Charlie Springfield asked.

'I can't ride on without a horse, can I?' Spike Ovenwood argued.

'That's easy fixed,' Mingo said, giving Sarah a suggestive wink. 'We could leave you right here until the Big Bad Wolf comes to gobble you up.'

That caused a laugh all round, except that Spike Ovenwood was not amused. The balloon of his ego had been truly pricked and he was fuming with resentment.

'Tell you what we do,' Cal Livermore said. He gestured with his canteen from which he was drinking. 'We just sit right here and let the Big Bad Wolf you mentioned come to us. That's what we do.'

A silence descended on the group. Mingo was looking at Sarah and he shook his black beard at her. Sarah knew then that the dancing had been about: Mingo wanted her for himself. Apart from being repelled by this big bear of a man, this had other implications she would need to work out.

'Listen, Cal,' Tod Ridelle said, 'we can't sit here for ever.'

Livermore held up his canteen again. 'Why not? We've got blankets against the cold. We've got stuff to eat. There's plenty of cover up there in the rocks. This is a better situation than that old ruined cabin. We all hated it, anyway. That's why we burned it down.' He paused. 'What we do is just sit tight here and watch and wait, and soon enough that bounty hunter who calls himself Horse Soldier will fall like a ripe plum right into our laps.'

There was another reflective silence and no one raised his voice to disagree. Mingo grinned at Sarah from under his Stetson and Spike Ovenwood's ego started to reinflate.

The question Horse Soldier was turning over in his mind was, What do I do next? Do I ride on in pursuit of those desperadoes, or do I see that Clemy is taken care of?

'What you do now?' Morello asked helpfully.

'We must rescue my ma,' Clemy said. That was her most important consideration, but she hadn't yet worked out the possible consequences.

Horse was trying to think of things from all angles. He guessed that Morello might be willing to escort Clemy back to Ed and Phoebe Potkin's place but he didn't feel able to trust Morello completely, so he dismissed that possibility from his mind.

While he was thinking he inspected Spike Ovenwood's horse and saw that, though it wasn't a thoroughbred, it was good enough. There was even a Winchester carbine in a saddle holster. Ovenwood must be boiling over with fury at losing that *and the girl too*! He drew the Winchester carbine from its sheath and examined it closely. It was probably the weapon that had wounded Running Deer.

'I know you can use this,' he said to Clemy. He had indeed taught her how to work the action of a similar Winchester just a year before and she had fired it at a tin can on the fence in the yard, missing it by inches. She might be capable of drawing it from the scabbard and warning off an enemy. Horse must take a chance on that.

'Tell you what you do,' he said to Clemy. 'You ride back to Phoebe's place and tell her how things are.'

'But I want to help to rescue Mummy,' Clemy protested.

'I know the best way to rescue your mother,' Horse Soldier said firmly, 'and I promise you I mean to do it.'

After that, Clemy agreed reluctantly and Horse and Morello watched her ride back in the direction of the ranch.

Doc Higgins was on the seat of the buckboard and Ed Potkin was sitting beside him with his leg strapped up. Sheriff Stafford was jogging alongside, looking important and Big Jim was on the other side of the buckboard looking somewhat diminutive on a horse that was big enough to make him look like a dwarf. Running Deer was back in Simm City under doctor's orders to rest up and keep out of trouble. Keeping out of trouble meant going into the saloon and ordering a beer. That old gossip Stan Balding was delighted to see him. It was always good to hear the chink of coins in his till and the rustle of dollar bills was even better.

'How's the shoulder?' Stan Balding asked him.

'You want the truth, it's aching like hell,' Running Deer replied. 'Like it's been hit by a sledge hammer and it's just become aware of the fact.'

'That's too bad,' Stan Balding said. 'Like when there was a shoot-out one time here in the bar. That was before Sheriff Stafford's time. Some old miner lost his shirt in a game of poker and drew a gun and started shooting every whichway. I ducked down behind this here bar just in time to avoid getting one right here between the eyes.' Balding pointed to the spot in the middle of his forehead where the bullet might have struck. 'Blasted some of my best whiskey to hell and back,' he added. 'Enough to put the big fish to sleep for ever and a day!'

'If that bullet had hit you you wouldn't have felt a damned thing,' Running Deer said. 'You'd have been stone cold dead, so it doesn't figure.'

Stan Balding couldn't reason well so he just shrugged. 'Anyway, what's the news with that kidnapping? Are those scaramouches claiming some sort of reward?'

'You know damned well they are,' Running Deer said disagreeably. 'They want Horse Soldier dead. That's what they want.'

'Too bad you got yourself shot,' Stan Balding said tactlessly. 'And it ain't right kidnapping that woman and that girl. Sarah's a highly respectable woman and Clemy is a real nice girl. Everyone agrees with me on that.'

Running Deer had heard enough from that old cuss. So he took his beer over to the window and sat there nursing it. The poker players who had been listening to the con-

versation were all peering in Running Deer's direc-
tion.They had nothing much to do except drink and
gamble away their frugal dollars and they were glad of the
entertainment.

Running Deer sat at the window and watched the storm
blowing itself out across the plains.

'I've got to do something,' he muttered to himself. 'If I
sit here all day listening to that stupid drivelling old coot I
shall go plumb crazy in the head. I must damn well do
something, but what?'

When Doc Higgins got to the Potkin place the first thing
he saw was Phoebe staring out in all directions, no doubt
looking for her man. When she saw the buckboard she
made a sudden gesture of relief and exasperation and
came hurrying towards them.

'Thank the good Lord we got here!' Ed said. 'Phoebe
will be real mad when she sees me.'

'Don't you worry, Mrs Potkin,' Sheriff Stafford piped
up. 'Things aren't as bad as they seem.'

When Phoebe saw Ed Potkin sitting on the seat beside
Doc Higgins with his leg all strapped up she didn't know
whether to laugh or cry so she did a bit of both. 'You
damned old fool!' she cried out with relief. 'I told you you
were too old for this rushing and capering about. I've
been worried sick about you!'

Ed was trying not to laugh. He was so glad to be home,
but he was worried about Horse Soldier and Sarah and the
girl. Doc Higgins helped Ed down from the buckboard
and into the Potkins' rather stark hillbilly cabin. Ed told
Phoebe all that had happened, the way Horse Soldier had
crept up on the McMee place and killed one of the

kidnappers and how the kidnappers had afterwards
burned down the cabin and rode away to the hill country
with Sarah and Clemy still in their power.

'Oh, those poor creatures!' Phoebe wailed. 'Why
should this happen, and what's to become of them?'

As they were talking, Big Jim who had been looking out
across the plain suddenly turned. 'I see a horse!' he said,
'and there's a rider too. Looks like a small child.'

They all crowded on to the veranda and watched as
Clemy rode in on Spike Ovenwood's horse.

Horse Soldier and Morello were riding across the plain to
the more hummocky area where the kidnappers were
holed up with Sarah. Horse knew exactly where they were.
He had been there frequently and had once taken both
Sarah and Clemy there. It had been christened
Scrambling Rocks by the Indians way back and the name
fitted it perfectly.

'You know that place?' Morello asked Horse.

'Sure, I know it,' Horse said. 'It's like a fortress. Plenty
of places to hide up and shoot down at anyone approaching.'

'Can we creep without them seeing?' Morello asked.

'Not very likely,' Horse said, 'unless you're a coyote or a
wolf. And then it would have to be in the dark.'

'We wait for night time?' Morello suggested.

'I don't think so,' Horse told him. 'Best you ride back
to Simm City like I told you. I have to do this on my own.'

'What you do?' Morello asked him suspiciously. 'You
give yourself up to those evil *hombres*, they kill you, Mr
Horse.'

'That's as maybe,' Horse replied. 'A man lives until he

102

dies. Like the Indians say, it's written in the stars.'

Morello raised his eyebrows in surprise. 'I come with you,' he insisted. 'Maybe we both written in the stars.'

Horse shrugged his shoulders and rode on.

In an hour they saw the Scrambling Rocks pushing up from the plain, shelf upon shelf, rock upon rock, gleaming hard and surprisingly beautiful but terribly relentless in the glaring sun.

Vic Ridelle had climbed up to a good vantage point high among the rocks and, as he peered out through his field glasses, he saw the two approaching riders. 'I see him!' he shouted. 'Horse Soldier. He's coming right towards us like a deer coming to a creek ready to be killed.'

'Like a prisoner walking right up to the noose,' Spike Ovenwood intervened. 'Give me your Winchester,' he said to Gus Daniel. 'He comes a bit closer I can take him out with no trouble at all.'

'You damned fool!' Gus Daniel shouted back. 'We don't want him dead, not yet, anyway. We want to blow him away in our own good time. Why can't you get your numbskull head around that?'

'Wait a minute, there's someone with him,' Vic Ridelle said, still peering through his glasses. 'He's wearing a Mexican sombrero. They're coming in together.'

'Then why don't I take out the Mexican?' Spike Ovenwood suggested. 'Blow that sombrero right off his head and the greaser's head with it. Then we take care of Horse Soldier.'

Neither Cal Livermore nor Vic Ridelle had any objection to that. In fact, Cal Livermore thought of it as a kind of humorous refinement. 'Give him the Winchester, Gus, since he wants to kill so bad. It's time we had some fun.'

Gus Daniel wasn't a man to surrender his weapons easily. He took pride in the Winchester and looked after it like a father cares for his children. 'If someone has to kill the Mexican with my Winchester it has to be me,' he said resolutely.

'OK, you do it,' Vic Ridelle said. 'We'll just set here and watch the fun.'

Sarah was half concealed in a little crevice. She had been secretly working to cut her bonds against a sharp stone without being noticed and while this shouted argument bounced to and fro among the rocks she took the chance to work even harder.

The only one close enough to detect her was the big bear Mingo and he was chuckling away to himself and appeared to be enjoying the debate. When he glanced at Sarah out of the corner of his eye and gave another wink she shuddered with apprehension. Thank the Lord Clemy got away, she thought.

'They're going to kill Horse,' she said quietly to Mingo.

Mingo grinned. 'I don't think so, not yet, anyway. But I wouldn't place bets on that Mexican's life. If Ovenwood gets his way, that *hombre* will be dead meat in just a minute from now.'

'Stop right here!' Horse said to Morello.

They both reined in. 'Why we stop?' Morello asked him.

Horse shook his head. 'I want you to get yourself out of the line of fire,' Horse said. 'Those murdering critters want me alive. D'you understand that? They don't give a damn about you and you're within range of those

Winchesters. Why don't you just drop back and get yourself out of range, and let me do the rest?'

'I don't leave you like this,' Morello protested. 'I here
to help you. You want to offer yourself like the sheep in the
slaughter. The shepherd does not leave the sheep. The
shepherd rescues the sheep.'

'That may be in the Good Book but it doesn't mention
putting yourself in the line of fire,' Horse Soldier retorted.

Morello didn't have time to take Horse up on that
because at that moment there was a bang and a flash from
the rocks and Morello rose from the saddle as though he
was about to speak and then fell back from his horse's
back on to the stony plain.

Big Jim was small but he had a big heart and the courage
of a lion. He had worked with Morello on the ranches and
he had a high regard for him. Meeting him again in Simm
City had been a matter of good fortune and, now that
Morello had fallen in with Horse Soldier, Big Jim had a
feeling of increased obligation. If Morello was involved in
a rescue attempt he wanted to be there too.

After he had listened to Clemy's story he spoke up suddenly. 'Listen,' he said to the others. 'I don't know about
you guys, but I'm going to ride out and do all I can to help
Horse Soldier and my buddy Morello.'

Sheriff Stafford looked at him in some surprise. He
thought that the bigger a man was the braver he should
be. He was in fact of middling height himself and liked to
keep out of trouble. Big Jim wasn't exactly a midget but
neither was he a man you would usually take more than a
second glance at.

Clemy had spoken about Scrambling Rocks and the

Potkins were well acquainted with that feature. Despite his fractured leg Ed Potkins would have been only too pleased to get into the saddle and guide them up to Scrambling Rocks. But Phoebe brought her foot down on that one.

'You're not going anywhere,' she said abruptly. 'You're staying right here and resting up. You've done more than enough tearing around and nearly getting yourself killed as it is.'

Then Clemy spoke up again. 'I wanted to stay up there and help my pa rescue my ma. So if anybody wants to go up there I want to show him the way.'

Everyone looked astonished and uneasy. 'But, Clemy,' Phoebe protested, 'you've just been through a terrible, rough ordeal and you're not fit to go anywhere.'

'I'd go to Hell and back to rescue my ma,' Clemy protested.

Doc Higgins had said nothing so far. He knew that Phoebe was right about Ed Potkins and, though he admired the child for her determination, he thought she was wrong to put herself in jeopardy.

He turned to his drinking pal. 'You must know the Scrambling Rocks, Staff. Why don't you lead a posse out there and we can sort this muddle out before it gets any worse?'

Sheriff Stafford wasn't over keen on the idea. Going to the Scrambling Rocks would mean bloodshed and he hated to see blood pouring out of a dying man.

But now everyone was looking in his direction and the onus was on him.

'OK,' he shrugged. 'We go up there and see what we can do.' In fact, though he knew about Scrambling Rocks he had never actually seen the place; this was, in his opinion, a mighty tricky situation.

Then Clemy spoke up again. 'I want to be part of the posse. I want to lead you there for the sake of my ma and pa,' she pleaded.

Phoebe Potkin had known Clemy since she was a tiny child and she had grown to think of her as the daughter she had never had. She was fond of Sarah too, in her own way. If she had been a man Phoebe would have been glad to lead them to Scrambling Rocks herself. But again she urged caution. 'That's a might tricky situation up there,' she warned. 'A man could scramble about for a week without being caught. That's what they say.'

Doc Higgins was the most respected person in the party. He had brought most of Simm City's children into the world. He had treated their ailments and fixed their broken bones and everyone looked up to him.

'Tell you what, good folk,' he said. 'I know we all want Mrs Millar to be rescued without harm to her husband. I suggest you lead the way, Sheriff, and I'll follow on my buckboard. If Clemy insists on coming she can ride with me.'

'Well, I can ride the buckboard too,' Ed Potkin said. 'That way I won't use my busted leg. And I can use a gun as well as any man.'

'Don't be such a cussed old fool!' Phoebe piped up.

But the matter was quickly settled. Big Jim and the sheriff would ride ahead and Clemy and the doctor would follow at a somewhat slower pace on the buckboard.

Sarah gasped when she heard the shot and saw Morello fall from the saddle.

'You've killed an innocent man!' she said to Gus Daniel.

107

'No one here is innocent,' Gus Daniel shouted back. 'That greaser stuck his nose in where it wasn't wanted and got it squeezed. That's what happens when you stick your nose into other people's business.'

'You aimed too low,' Spike Ovenwood jeered. 'Look you got him in the chest. You want the head, you aim higher.'

Gus Daniel looked out and saw a number of things all at once. Morello's horse was rearing and prancing. Horse Soldier had reached out and grabbed its bridle to steady it. And the stricken man was writhing on the ground.

'You didn't kill the man!' Spike Ovenwood said. 'Give me your gun and I'll take another shot. If you aim to kill a man you do it properly like I said.'

'OK, big shot!' Gus Daniel growled. 'You want to do it, you do it.' He handed Spike Ovenwood his precious Winchester.

When the first shot came and knocked Morello dean off his horse, Horse grabbed the horse instinctively and pulled it round to cover Morello. Then he turned his attention to the wounded man.

Morello was conscious and there was blood welling from the wound in his chest where he had been hit high in the ribcage. Now he was gasping and struggling to get to his feet.

'Hold still!' Horse knelt beside him and examined the wound. He saw that the bullet had struck the bone and ricocheted away, leaving a bloody gash. Half an inch lower and it might have passed between the ribs and struck the lungs or the heart. An inch or two higher it might have struck Morello right in the throat.

'Am I dead man?' Morello gasped.

'I think you'll live if I can get you under cover,' Horse Soldier told him.

The trouble was there was no cover, just a little cluster of boulders about ten feet away.

'Can you crawl?' Horse Soldier asked him.

'I crawl,' Morello muttered between his teeth.

'I'll cover you.' Morello drew his own Winchester.

The next moment Spike Ovenwood took his second shot. He had aimed high to judge the trajectory. It was a matter of some pride and killing Morello was like punching Daniel right on the nose. It was a difficult shot since Horse Soldier was behind Morello's horse to keep him covered. Spike Ovenwood rose a little higher so that he could put a bullet over the horse and kill Morello as he crawled frantically for cover.

Horse Soldier could see Ovenwood rising higher and taking aim. He breathed in, held his breath and took careful aim as Spike Ovenwood's shot whined in. Then he raised his Winchester to judge the trajectory and squeezed the trigger.

Spike Ovenwood turned to Gus Daniel with a grin and said. 'You see him crawl? That was a difficult shot. Now I'm going to put one right in his back and finish the job.'

But Ovenwood never got to finishing that job. Horse Soldier's bullet caught him right between the teeth. His head jerked back, he made an inarticulate gurgling noise and choked on his own blood.

Gus Daniel stared at him aghast, thinking, My Gawd, that might have been me! Mingo was squatting in a cave a few feet away. 'Got him right in the teeth,' he said in astonishment. 'That was some lucky shot!'

109

That wasn't luck, Gus Daniel thought: that was real shooting. Now he knew more than ever what they were up against.

Cal Livermore and Vic Ridelle had been watching from further up in the rocks and they were equally impressed. They had heard of Horse Soldier's skill with a gun but this was something else again! Charlie Springfield had never seen anything like it. Why have I got myself into this, he thought? For just a handful of dollars too! Now there are only five of us. Five of us against one. Maybe we should just let the woman go and light out before this skookum gets right in among us and takes us all to hell!

Sarah was still sawing away at her bonds and she was almost down to the last thread. What could she do next? she wondered. When Spike Ovenwood gargled and fell back she didn't have time to be sorry. He was one of the worst of her captors. But she knew that Horse Soldier was in great danger. She had seen Morello fall back and crawl away to the pile of rocks and she hoped he and Horse Soldier were safe, at least for the moment. She noticed that Mingo seemed strangely unconcerned. He was even chuckling to himself.

'That damned fool deserved all he got,' he said quietly, as though he was on her husband's side.

If I make a break now, I might just get away. Then I might save us both, Sarah thought.

Horse Soldier had drawn back with the horses. He knew he had hit Spike Ovenwood, but he wasn't quite sure whether he was wounded or dead. Now he hobbled the horses together and bent over Morello.

'You kill the *hombre*?' Morello asked him, gritting his

teeth with pain.

'A lucky shot,' Horse said. He had taken a dressing from his saddle-bag and he held it against Morello's wound. Morello winced with pain.

'Hold this against your wound to stop the bleeding, and drink this.' He pressed a small bottle to Morello's lips. 'Take it slowly,' he said.

'Will I be to die?' Morello asked him.

'One day,' Horse said. 'But not today. The bullet bounced off you. You were only just within range. Could have cracked a rib, but I think you're going to be OK. Just lie still and think about the girl you left behind in Mexico.'

Morello was in too much pain to laugh.

When Horse Soldier looked out over the rock, he saw someone waving a dirty white bandanna. Someone was calling out to him but it was a little too far off to make out the words.

He checked his Winchester, released his horse, and mounted up. He rode forward until he was close enough to hold a shouted conversation with the kidnappers. It was Cal Livermore who had spoken. Now he spoke again.

'Listen, Horse,' Livermore shouted. 'You come because you want to see your woman. Is that right?'

'You know damned well that's right,' Horse Soldier shouted back. 'I want her free, you know that.'

Now another voice spoke up. It was Vic Ridelle. 'We don't want your woman, Horse. We want you.'

Horse took a deep breath. 'You let me see Sarah's safe and sound,' he shouted, 'I'll give myself up.'

'That's a deal,' Vic Ridelle hollered back.

Horse Soldier extended his arms, still holding his

Winchester in his right hand. 'Well, I'm here,' he said. 'You bring Sarah to me and as soon as I know she's good and safe, I'll surrender myself.'

There was a moment of tense silence and then suddenly Horse Soldier heard Sarah's voice. 'Don't give yourself up, Mike!' she cried frantically. 'These men mean to torture you to death.'

Up in the Scrambling Rocks someone gave a grim laugh.

Horse Soldier now knew that Sarah was alive. Clemy was safe and Sarah was alive. That was all that mattered to him. But would she stay alive? That was the big question.

'What do you want for me to do?' Horse Soldier shouted to the kidnappers.

'What *you* do is you drop your gun, unbuckle your gunbelt, and walk right up with your hands above your head. Then we release your woman and she can take your horse and ride away. This is Cal Livermore speaking, and we figure that's a fair deal.' Horse remembered Livermore's brother, one of the men he had had to kill up at the James place in the Badlands in New Mexico.

'That's OK by me,' he said, 'you bring my wife Sarah right up to me, then we make the exchange.'

'Just as long as you drop your weapons, that's the deal,' Cal Livermore said.

Horse Soldier threw down his Winchester and waited.

'Now you unbuckle your gunbelt and let it drop. Then kick it away. It's not much good to you anyway, now,' Cal Livermore said in a high gloating tone.

Horse Soldier did as he was told. When he had kicked the gunbelt away he could almost hear the sigh of relief and satisfaction from the Scrambling Rocks. 'Now it's your turn,' he shouted.

For a moment nothing happened. He knew the kid-nappers wanted to kill him but they were divided in their opinion about how it should be done. He could hear voices from the rocks. Cal Livermore and Vic Ridelle were arguing with Gus Daniel and Charlie Springfield. Livermore and Ridelle wanted Horse Soldier's head on a plate and the other two were in favour of shooting him down right there while he was unarmed.

Sarah had freed her hands. All she had to do now was to get them on a weapon and use it.

Mingo said nothing but he had his head cocked on one side, listening to the debate. Then he leered sideways at Sarah. 'They want to kill your old man,' he said quietly. 'You want to save him?'

Sarah nodded. What a ridiculous question. Of course she wanted to save him!

'OK,' Mingo said. 'I'll make a deal with you. I'll help you save him: you come with me.'

Sarah stared at him aghast. What could he be implying? 'Come with you?' she said.

'That's what I said. You promise to come with me. I save Horse. That's the deal. Everyone comes out of this alive.'

Sarah could hardly believe her ears. This repulsive bear of a man was actually asking her to ride off with him and leave her husband to his fate!

But before she could reply a voice spoke from above. 'Mingo, you just take the woman across to Horse Soldier and make the exchange. And you, Charlie, go with them.'

'OK,' Mingo said to Sarah. 'You do as I say, everything's going to be all right.'

Charlie Springfield rose from behind a rock, He was

113

none too pleased about walking out to meet Horse Soldier, especially with Mingo, a man who, he thought, was no more to be trusted than a cage of monkeys. So he drew his shooter and held it ready.

'So you freed your hands,' Mingo said to Sarah. 'That's good. Makes things easier. You walk ahead and do as you're bid; everything's going to be OK.'

Then the three of them, Sarah, Mingo, and Charlie Springfield walked out from the Scrambling Rocks to meet Horse Soldier.

CHAPTER EIGHT

As Sarah walked towards Horse she felt faint with fear. What is going to happen next? she wondered. Mingo was right behind her and she could feel his gun pressing against her back. Charlie Springfield was behind her too, slightly to the left, and she sensed from his quick breathing that he was, to say the least, somewhat nervous. When a man is nervous he gets jumpy and if he has a gun in his hand anything might happen.

She could see Horse Soldier getting closer. He had his hands held high and he was staring at her with a mixture of anxiety and concern.

'Are you OK, Sarah?' he asked quietly.

'Don't worry about me,' she said.

'OK, now we stop,' Mingo said.

They came to a stop a few feet away from one another and each saw what they feared to see. Sarah's clothes had been worn away to rags and Horse had a sprouting unkempt beard and his red-rimmed eyes were wild with anxiety.

Horse nodded. He wanted to reach out to Sarah and verify that she was really there. 'Now, I want to see my wife safely on a horse,' he said to Mingo. 'Then you can do what you like with me.'

Horse turned his gaze on Charlie Springfield and saw the fear and uneasiness in his eyes. He noted that the Colt in his right hand was shaking slightly. 'Are you one of the execution squad?' he asked.

Charlie Springfield seemed to pull himself together. 'I'm just doing what I'm paid to do.'

'A paid killer,' Horse reflected. 'I hope the pay is good.' He turned to Mingo. 'OK, let's get it over with. What's the next move?'

'Like you said, your woman Sarah mounts up on your horse and then she's free.'

Horse Soldier nodded and gave him a wry grin. 'Let me see that.'

Mingo gestured to Charlie Springfield. 'Charlie, bring the man's horse over, will you?'

Charlie Springfield looked a little uncertain, but then he holstered his shooter and walked over to retrieve Horse's mount.

'That's a mighty fine hoss, you got there,' Mingo said.

'Best of the bunch,' Horse Soldier admitted.

'Help the lady up on to the hoss, will you, Charlie?' Mingo said.

Charlie Springfield grabbed hold of Sarah's arm but Sarah pulled away. 'I'm not going without my husband!' she said.

'Do as the man says,' Horse said.

Charlie Springfield helped Sarah into the saddle.

'Now bring the other hoss over, will you, Charlie?'

'What the hell for?' Charlie Springfield asked.

'Just because I ask you to.' Mingo gave a harsh unmusical laugh.

Charlie Springfield went over and gathered Morello's horse. He saw Morello lying behind the pile of rocks. 'You still alive?' he said.

Morello groaned.

Charlie Springfield led the horse back to Mingo.

'Thank you, Charlie,' Mingo said graciously. 'Now maybe you'll help me to mount up too.'

Charlie Springfield stared at Mingo aghast. 'You ain't going anywhere, Mingo.'

'That's what you think,' Mingo said. He mounted Morello's horse with surprising agility for such a big man and turned with his gun in his hand.

Horse Soldier had seen what was coming. He might have dived towards his Winchester or made a grab for this gunbelt, but they were well out of reach. Charlie Springfield, however, knew that he had been duped and he reacted instinctively. He drew his single-action Colt and made to cock it but he was just a second too slow. Mingo discharged his shooter right in Springfield's face. Springfield jerked back and lay twitching on the ground with an expression of astonishment in his dying eyes.

'Don't mess with Mingo,' Mingo said to the corpse. 'And don't follow,' he said to Horse. 'If you follow I might have to do the same to your woman and you wouldn't want to see her blasted to Kingdom Come, would you?'

Sarah was about to spur her mount away but Mingo grabbed her bridle and pulled it tight. Then he dug his heels into his horse's side and they galloped off.

'What the hell!' Morello gasped, raising his gun and firing. The shot whined close to Mingo but Morello was too weak and the bullet flew harmlessly into the air.

*

'Well, dang my hide!' Gus Daniel roared from his position among the Scrambling Rocks. 'Mingo killed Charlie and rode away with the woman!' Daniel was something of a fatalist but this was too amazing to believe!

Vic Ridelle was slithering and sliding down the rocks. 'That double-crossing rat!" he shouted. He came to rest close to the edge of the rocks and levered his Winchester. He knew that it was of little use firing at Mingo since Mingo was already already nothing but a smudge on the landscape, but he fired a shot anyway to express his frustration.

But now Cal Livermore came sliding down the rocks to join him. 'Save your bullets!' he said. 'Mingo got away with the woman but we've still got Horse Soldier in our sights. That's what we want, isn't it?'

He had spent long nights dreaming of Horse Soldier swinging from a lonely tree, but there was no lonely tree available and it was three against one. So it would have to do.

Horse Soldier had dropped to a kneeling position and he was levering his Winchester.

Livermore knew he was just within range and Horse Soldier knew how to handle his weapon. He could easily judge the angle and lob one right down on a man's head. Spike Ovenmore's smashed face was evidence of that. Yet Livermore prided himself on his shooting too. 'Spread out, boys,' he said. 'We go out to get him. When I give the order, we all fire at once. He won't know who to choose and, while he's deciding, we'll blast him full of holes.'

That was literally true since Vic Ridelle's favoured weapon was a scattergun.

*

Horse Soldier had retrieved his gunbelt and jerked his Colt free. He stuck it through his belt and waited as the three men spread out against the Scrambling Rocks. As they stared at him he checked each one of them with slow calculation. They were the most dangerous of the bunch. Which one should I go for? he asked himself.

Cal Livermore was in the middle with his Winchester held high. He could lower it in a instant and blast off a shot. To his right, Gus Daniel already had his gun pointing out towards Horse Soldier. Vic Ridelle, to Cal Livermore's left, had his scattergun ready and it would be deadly at close range.

If I'm going to die, which one do I take with me first? Horse thought. He fixed on Livermore and saw that Livermore wanted his blood most.

Vic Ridelle moved out to the right so that he was at least six feet away from Livermore. And Daniel moved out warily to the left.

What does a man do?

Suddenly his mind shifted to Sarah being forced by Mingo to ride away with him. With each wasted moment they were getting further and further off. And he was squandering his time. What would happen to Sarah when he lay dead in the dust?

Rage suddenly boiled up like a foaming cauldron. He swung his Winchester from the hip and fired. Cal Livermore was about to give the order to fire when the bullet caught him high on the chest. He staggered back but didn't fall. He managed to discharge his Winchester before he dropped on to one knee.

Gus Daniel levelled his gun and fired at Horse Soldier's head. But Horse Soldier was already halfway down and levering his Winchester. Daniel's bullet came so close that Horse felt it lift his Stetson and crease his scalp.

'Go down to Hell!' he shouted, as Daniel levelled his gun for a second shot.

Now Vic Ridelle came at a run towards him.

That scattergun is going to pepper me full of holes, Horse thought as he rolled to one side and fired.

Vic Ridelle stumbled but the bullet had gone wide.

Then came Daniel's second shot and it struck Horse's Winchester, casting it away.

This is it! Horse Soldier thought. Between them, I'm a dead man!

Cal Livermore was still alive and he was levering his Winchester for another shot. Daniel was running in, getting closer and closer, for a third shot. And Vic Ridelle came on relentlessly with that deadly scattergun.

Horse made a grab for his Colt. But would he be too late?

Everything seemed to happen in slow motion. Vic Ridelle was shouting a bloodcurdling war cry; Cal Livermore was crawling forward on his knees with a Colt in his hand, and Daniel was levelling his Winchester for the final shot!

Then fate intervened suddenly. There was a shot and it didn't come from Daniel. Daniel threw up his arms and dropped his gun and fell convulsing to the ground. Vic Ridelle swung away and discharged the scattergun into the air.

A short man stepped out from behind the Scrambling Rocks. It was Big Jim!

The little band with the buckboard driven by Doc Higgins

was quite close when they heard the shots.

'Dang my eyeballs!' Ed Potkins said to the doc. The shooting's started. I should be there! Those poor kids are in danger! Stop the buckboard. Get me on my horse! I've got to do what I can to save them!' He was so frantic that he was ready to hop off the buckboard and on to a horse, busted leg or not.

Clemy was frantic too. 'I must save my ma and pa!' she shouted.

Sheriff Stafford said nothing much at all. Perhaps he thought he should have ridden on with Big Jim.

Big Jim was a tenacious little *hombre*. As soon as he had seen the Scrambling Rocks rearing up from the plain he had decided to ride on ahead by a circular route. If his *amigo* Morello was in trouble he wanted to be right there to help him.

Horse Soldier staggered to his feet with his six shooter ready. But there wasn't much to do. Cal Livermore lay on his face, panting and groaning. Gus Daniel had fallen back with a hole in his head delivered by Big Jim's Winchester. The only one who was still alive was Vic Ridelle who was standing with his hands in the air and his scattergun at his feet.

Big Jim walked over and inspected the scene. 'Three dead and one shitting his pants,' he said, prodding Vic Ridelle in the side with his gun. 'You make a single move and you'll be as dead as these stiffs,' he threatened. 'Just lie down there with your face to the sod and you might just survive.'

Ridelle lay down as he was told and he was crying out of sheer frustration. Big Jim bent over him, relieved him of his Remington, sniffed at it, and hurled it away. 'You won't have any more use for that, my *amigo*!' he said.

He walked over to Horse Soldier and placed his hand on his arm. 'Are you OK, partner?' he enquired.

Horse Soldier nodded. 'Seems I'm alive,' he said sardonically.

'Amen to that!' The voice came from a small pile of rocks between twenty and thirty feet away.

Big Jim looked across and saw Morello trying to struggle to his feet. 'Ah, *amigo*,' he said. 'You seem to have taken one in the chest. Keep yourself quiet and still. The doctor man is on his way.'

As soon as Clemy saw her father she leaped down from the buckboard and ran to him. 'Daddy, Daddy, you're hurt!' she cried.

Horse Soldier had blood stinging his eye and realized he had been hit. The bullet had gone clean through his Stetson and carried it away. He knew the blood on his head made him look like a man from the Red Planet but he figured it couldn't be as bad as it looked. 'Don't worry, I'm OK,' he said.

'Where's my ma?' Clemy said, looking about her. When she saw the corpses of Cal Livermore and Gus Daniel and Spike Ovenwood she held her hands to her mouth in horror.

Doc Higgins had got off the buckboard and he said, 'Now, Miss Clementine, I want you to just go and sit on the buckboard and talk to Mr Potkin, keep him from jumping about and damaging his injured leg.'

'But I want to know what happened to my ma!' she pleaded.

'Ma's OK,' Horse Soldier told her.

'Where is she? I don't see her!' Clemy insisted.

Horse Soldier had no alternative; he had to tell her the truth that Mingo had forced her to ride away with him. He didn't mention that it was at gun point but Clemy had grown up a lot in the past few days. So she guessed what had happened.

'What are we going to do?' she cried. 'That man Mingo is evil!'

Horse Soldier didn't need telling that. What he needed was a reliable horse to ride after them in pursuit. 'I'm going after them. Your ma will be all right,' he said.

'I'm coming with you!' Clemy shouted. 'Give me a gun and a horse and I'll ride with you!'

'Now Miss Clementine, chasing after bad men is not for a lady,' Doc Higgins tried to soothe her. 'I'm sure we can manage to rescue your mother. You have to be ready to welcome her when she returns.'

The doc had now cleaned the blood from Horse Soldier's head and he looked almost human again. 'Don't fret yourself unduly,' Horse Soldier said to Clemy. 'I'm going to ride right after them and bring her back.'

Big Jim had been tending Morello and now Doc Higgins went to examine the gash on Morello's chest. 'Not too deep,' he said. 'I think you're set to live a little while longer,' he told Morello.

Morello gritted his teeth. 'I want to ride with Horse Soldier and get that big gorilla!' he declared.

'I advise you to get on the buckboard with the other walking wounded. A badly wounded man isn't going to be much good against a man like that Mingo.'

*

Sheriff Stafford decided he had to do something useful. So he took Vic Ridelle into custody. 'I'm taking you back to Simm City,' he said, 'so you can be put on trial and face the consequences.'

Vic Ridelle said nothing as Big Jim tied his hands behind his back. How had things gone so disastrously wrong? he was wondering. He knew the answer, too. How stupid to have pitched up at that half-ruined cabin! They should have taken the girl and the woman right back to New Mexico with them. The fact that Mingo had turned traitor and ridden off with the woman was no consolation at all. The other kidnappers were now as dead as spiked steers and it had all come to nothing. But he wouldn't be in custody for long. This Sheriff Stafford was nothing but mouth and his mouth didn't amount to much either.

Having tied up Ridelle's hands real tight, Big Jim watched as Horse Soldier went across to the Scrambling Rocks to pick out a horse. It wouldn't be as good as the horse Mingo had stolen, but it would have to do. Supplies too! Mingo had made off with his supplies.

When he had picked out Cal Livermore's horse he led it out and took a better look at it. Cal Livermore took care of his horses; that was the only thing in his favour. Some men would have been superstitious about riding a dead man's horse, but Horse Soldier wasn't too particular. All he wanted was to get after Mingo while the trail was still clear and do what he had to do to rescue Sarah.

When he looked round he saw that the little man, Big Jim, was already in the saddle, looking down at him.

'You going somewhere?' Horse asked him.

'Sure; I'm going with you,' Big Jim said. 'You going to rescue your wife from that guy who took her you need someone riding along with you. That makes sense, don't it?'

Horse Soldier was checking Cal Livermore's saddle-bag. Yes, there were supplies, enough maybe for three or four days. Horse was something of a loner. So he hesitated for a second.

'Better than talking to yourself or the stars,' Big Jim said. 'A man can go crazy that way especially if his kin is in danger. And I can see in the dark too. When the moon comes out it won't be too difficult to keep tracks on that kidnapping skunk.'

Horse twisted his mouth in a wry grin. He had always liked a man with a sense of humour. 'OK,' he said, 'you trail along, only don't talk too much and don't sing. A man who sings on the trail is a nuisance and a distraction.'

Horse Soldier swung up into the saddle and walked his horse over to where Doc Higgins had just finished examining the corpses.

'So you're going?' Doc Higgins asked him.

'I'm going,' Horse affirmed. 'There's nobody else can rescue Sarah.'

Doc Higgins nodded. He thought it was his friend the sheriff's duty, but he knew that Stafford, though good company for a drink in the saloon, was not a fighting man and probably should have been shooting pool in the saloon.

Mingo was riding Horse Soldier's horse with Sarah a little way ahead riding Morello's.

'Nice pieces of horseflesh we have here,' the big man said.

'Where are you taking me?' Sarah asked him over her shoulder.

'I'm taking you to a place you'll be happier than you've ever been in your fife before,' Mingo laughed.

'I don't think so,' Sarah said. 'You want me to be happy, you'll turn me loose right now.'

'Come now, that's no way to talk to a gentleman,' Mingo said. 'Maybe you didn't notice, but what I did back there was rescue you from death. I'm sure that man who calls himself Horse Soldier and claims to be your husband is glad you're still alive.'

They were trotting along not too fast across the scrubby plain and the light was already beginning to fade. It wouldn't be long before sundown and Sarah was trying to assess her position and decide what to do next.

'Look at it like this,' Mingo said, drawing up beside her. 'Horse Soldier is no real husband to you. He spends most of his time away from home on a bounty hunt, so you're already like a widow, you know.' He gave a low rumbling laugh that sounded like thunder clouds gathering on a distant horizon. 'I aim to give you a better kind of life. You come along with me, we go to New Mexico, or maybe Arizona, or California, somewhere nobody will know us and we start a new life. I've got money stashed away and I'm going to invest in a new spread that will make your itsy bitsy place back there look like a miniature Japanese stone garden way back East.'

So that was what Mingo intended: Sarah was to become his woman and settle down with him! The thought of it made her want to vomit. But she forced herself to laugh.

'You think you can get away with that nonsense?' she said.

'We are getting away with it, baby,' he chuckled. 'When the sun goes down we ride on. Nobody is going to catch us. By sun-up tomorrow we'll be too far ahead for anyone to catch us.'

That's what you think, Sarah thought.

Horse Soldier and Big Jim were cantering side by side. It wasn't difficult to follow the trail left by Mingo and Sarah so they made reasonably good progress. Where there was a difficulty Big Jim dismounted and examined the trail. He was obviously a master in the art of tracking which impressed Horse Soldier considerably.

Every so often they came upon a small object that Sarah had dropped on the trail, a piece of fabric, a button from a blouse; little things that were like messages in a bottle, saying, 'this way, this way . . . come and rescue me'.

'I figure they'll ride on through the night,' Horse Soldier said.

Big Jim disagreed. 'I don't think so. That horse of yours will need to rest up. A big man like Mingo on it's back it will need to have time to get its breath and eat some. You drive a horse too hard it's going to die on you. You know that.'

Horse knew that well enough but he was thinking desperately about Sarah. He was wondering how well Mingo knew the country and which way they might ride.

Mingo had in fact ridden that way more than once before and he remembered many of the bluffs and gulches. They were riding into brasada country, a land of almost impenetrable brush, mesquite, stunted pine, and juniper where maverick steers that had escaped might melt into the background and where a man could hide out for more than a year without being found. And that was what Mingo was counting on. When they got clean away he intended to make Sarah his woman. He had decided that as soon as he had seen her when they abducted her and Clemy from the ranch and he had waited for the right moment to make his move.

'You don't want to worry about your old man,' he said to Sarah. 'He hasn't a hope in hell of finding you in this wild country.'

'If Horse is looking for us, he'll find us wherever we go,' Sarah retorted.

It was now almost dark but she knew the moon would be rising quite soon. She pictured her husband riding on through the gloom and knew that, sooner or later, he would need to stop and wait for the sun to come up again.

Now it was dark Doc Higgins was getting worried. Riding through the day was OK and he knew the way back to Simm City; at night it was a very different matter and Doc Higgins had no experience in being guided by the stars. In any case he had his patients to consider.

Clemy had been sitting there silent. She was as worried as hell about her ma and pa. But she suddenly shook her head. 'I know the way back,' she said. 'I can read the stars since I was nothing but a little kid. So, just give me the reins. The moon will be out soon. Then I can see every hill and tree.'

She sounded so confident that Doc Higgins was forced to give in. He was a psychologist and he figured taking the buckboard back to Simm City would help Clemy to keep her mind off her troubles.

It took half the night to get back, but the usual crowd of idlers and night birds were still roistering around and two men were going at it hammer and tongs outside Stan Balding's saloon.

Running Deer McVicar was standing on the sidewalk with his arm in a sling. When he saw the buckboard approaching, he ran down Main Street, expecting to see a number of corpses bumping along on the board, but all he saw was Doc Higgins and Morello who was groaning. Sheriff Stafford was riding alongside with Vic Ridelle in tow. Ridelle looked like a man in a nightmare but he said nothing.

The doc dropped Clemy and Ed Potkins off at the Potkins' spread. Doc Higgins had waited there just long enough to hear Phoebe Potkins giving Ed what she called *a big flea in his ear*!

As soon as Running Deer recognized Vic Ridelle he wanted to pull him down from his horse and maul him around, would have done so, too, if it hadn't been for his wounded shoulder.

Sheriff Stafford was looking proud, and even the roisterers stopped when they saw he had made an arrest. 'We got to get you in the caboose, my man!' he said somewhat boastfully to Ridelle.

'What happened to the rest of them?' Running Deer asked him.

'All lying there waiting for the coyotes and the buzzards to pick at their bones,' Stafford crowed as though he had despatched them personally.

' 'Cept for Mingo,' Morello corrected. 'Mingo made off with Horse's woman Sarah. Horse and Big Jim are riding in pursuit. Don't fancy their chances, though. Mingo might be six four and wide with it but he's the most slippery *hombre* I know.'

Running Deer looked more than a little disappointed. 'If I'd been there, that big *hombre* would be waiting for the coyotes to pick at him like the rest of them,' he said.

'We did what we had to do,' Stafford replied, as he urged Vic Ridelle on towards the caboose.

Ridelle's no pushover, Running Deer thought. He makes a prison break I've got to be there to shoot him down before he does any more harm to innocent folk!

The moon was riding high when Mingo decided it was time to stop. They were in a good position by a small creek, good for the horses too.

'We're going to stop here, lady,' he told Sarah. 'We have ourselves a little supper and turn in for the night. But I want you to watch yourself else I'll have to shoot you. Now we wouldn't want that, would we?' He sounded over-polite in his own greasy fashion, the sort of *hombre* you wouldn't trust any further than you could throw him, which, in Mingo's case, wouldn't be very far.

Sarah dismounted and took a good look around. Not much chance of escaping in this brush country. But if she could get to the horses she might make a break for it.

Mingo hobbled the horses and let them graze along the bank of the creek.

'Sorry to tell you I can't entertain you with a fire,' he said. 'We have to eat cold jerky, which ain't so bad for one night. When we get clean away, I'll promise you this: we'll have a real grand feast to celebrate our union. How would that be?' After that he gave a great bellowing laugh.

That same moon was riding high when Horse Soldier and Big Jim decided to stop. The spot they chose was on the edge of the brasada country and there was a narrow creek to water the horses.

They gathered dead branches together and made a fire.

'Mingo sees the fire, he'll know we're on our way,' Big Jim said.

There wasn't much to eat and most of it came from Big Jim's saddle-bag. Cal Livermore's saddle-bag contained very little, no bedroll, though there was a rather smelly blanket. Though there was a chill in the air, Horse Soldier decided to stretch out on the ground with his head resting on Cal Livermore's saddle. 'I don't think Livermore's likely to come up and haunt us,' he said.

It had been a long and stressful day and they needed all the rest they could get. The last thing he thought of was Sarah in the grip of that big bear but he had no time to reflect because he was asleep.

Sarah was bone tired too, but she couldn't sleep. Her mind was too busy whirring around like a windmill desperately trying to find a way out. When she did drop off for a moment she dreamed of a long driveway lined with trees that bent over her and whispered, 'Run like the wind! He's coming to get you.' She didn't stop to look back; she just ran on as fast as she could, but her legs felt like jelly and the breath of the monster was breathing like fire on the back of her neck. And then she woke.

The monster's breath had been Mingo's snores. He was asleep in Horse Soldier's bedroll with his face towards her. She was wrapped up in Morello's bedroll.

'I'm sure Horse won't begrudge me a good night's sleep in his bedroll,' Mingo had said earlier, and Sarah had shuddered. It was like an omen for the future.

'I hope a rattlesnake comes out at you in the night and bites you,' she said.

That had made Mingo laugh, his big unpleasant laugh. 'That's no nevermind to me,' he had jeered. 'The rattlers are my friends. I never had any trouble from them. I just talk to them and they slither away and leave me in peace.'

Now he was snoring like an elephant and Sarah was wide awake, considering her position.

Horse Soldier woke to the cry of coyotes. He too had been dreaming. In his dream a grizzly had been lumbering towards him with its teeth bared and its paws stretched out towards him. It was about to rip out his heart with those terrible razor-sharp talons. Horse was fumbling for his shooter but he couldn't find it. The next instant the grizzly would be on him and that would be his end. Horse had heard tell of mountain men who had wrestled with bears and killed them but he didn't give much credit to those far-fetched legends.

He got up from the ground and looked and listened and saw Big Jim staring at him from close by. In the light of the declining moon Big Jim was sitting by the remains of the fire, smoking a curly pipe.

'Thought I'd wait for you to wake,' Big Jim said, in a surprisingly deep voice for such a small man. 'I've got coffee going and a little bit of breakfast. It ain't much but it will keep us going until we catch up on that baboon.' He sounded cheerful and optimistic.

Horse joined him at the fire and accepted a mug of bitter-tasting coffee. He drank it down and immediately felt a whole lot better.

'It'll soon be sun-up,' Big Jim said. 'We should hit the

trail just as soon as maybe. Mingo will want to get going as soon as he can.'

'You ridden with Morello much?' Horse asked him. He was beginning to see Big Jim as a highly resourceful *hombre* who always looked on the bright side of things. A good buddy to have when you were in trouble.

'Oh, Morello and me go back a long ways,' Big Jim said. 'We were waddies together on ranches back in New Mexico where we're headed right now.' He got up, tipped the dregs of his coffee on the remains of the fire, and stubbed out his pipe. 'You don't smoke quirlies or a pipe?' he asked, as he started getting ready to strike camp.

'Couldn't take to it somehow,' Horse said. 'Seemed like a waste of money especially when a guy hasn't got much.'

'That's just when you need it,' Big Jim said.

They threw rocks and sand on the fire and brought the horses in.

'You figure they're far ahead?' Horse asked Big Jim.

'I figure we catch up on them just as long as we can pick up the trail,' Big Jim replied optimistically.

They mounted up and rode on.

The sun was already peeping up through the trees. If it had been a man it might have parted the branches and seen a big hulk of a man with his jeans halfway down his legs stooping and straining behind a tree. That was Mingo at his most vulnerable and Sarah knew it. Somehow she had succeeded in getting through the night, but it hadn't been easy. Once when she had got up stealthily and taken a step towards him, Mingo had stopped snoring and snapped open his eyes.

'Hello, Lady Beautiful,' he had said. 'You coming over

to join me in here? I've been keeping a place snug and warm for you.'

This was her second chance. Could she grab a gun or make a dash for it into the scrub? A man with his jeans round his ankles isn't going do much in the way of running, is he?

But then Sarah saw that Mingo had his horse tethered to a tree close by and in front of him lay his shooter. If only she could get to that shooter she could blast him out of existence. Then again, although Sarah was a good shot, she had never killed a man and had never wanted to. There must be some other way . . . but what?

CHAPTER NINE

Horse Soldier and Big Jim came upon the campsite after an hour. No sign of a fire.

'It must have been kind of chilly during the night,' Big Jim muttered, raking over the remains of the camp. 'They don't have much chow either. I figure a big man like Mingo gives great importance to his grub. When it comes to decision time, is his big belly or Sarah gonna be more important to him?'

'Well, he's not going to have Sarah and that's a given fact!' Horse Soldier said bluntly.

'What do we aim to do in the way of tactics, my friend?' Big Jim asked him. 'Do we just ride in on them and shoot the hell out of the guy, or do something a bit more clever?'

Horse Soldier couldn't supply an answer. During his time as a bounty hunter he had faced many difficult situations but none quite as tricky as this. 'I think we have to do what seems best at the time,' he said.

'And what's best for your good woman,' Big Jim agreed.

'When the time comes, I have to do this alone,' Horse Soldier added. 'I fix Mingo. You know I made a deal with him back in Simm City. We actually sat down and had a beer together outside Stan Balding's place. I should have blasted the hell out of him then and there, but he said I could count on him to free Sarah and Clemy at a certain price.'

'Well, maybe that's what he wants right now. He's making sure you keep your end of the bargain,' Big Jim suggested.

'I don't think so,' Horse Soldier said. 'I think he's trying to double-cross me and keep Sarah for himself.'

'That Sarah of yourn must be something of a woman. Like that gel the Greeks fought over in ancient times. I can't remember her name right now.'

'Well, she's a lot too good for a lump of blubber like Mingo,' Horse Soldier said.

'And we can't let him get away with it,' Big Jim said with some determination. 'Even if I have to kill him myself,' he added.

Back in Simm City, Vic Ridelle was lying on a very hard bunk in the city jail. Maybe the judge would come and he would be sentenced to death for killing a number of *hombres*. Should he just lie there and wait like a Christmas goose waiting for the axe to fall on his head before the Christmas feast? He didn't think so.

Sheriff Stafford was sitting at his desk out there in the office. He was doing paperwork, writing an account of the recent episode up at the Scrambling Rocks. Stafford was no William Shakespeare but, when it came to writing an account in which he figured as a hero of the law, he was no slouch. He compared himself in his imagination to William Butler Hickock of Deadwood or Wyatt Earp of Tombstone. Preferably Wyatt Earp since he survived!

'Can you spell?' he threw at Vic Ridelle over his shoulder.

'I did learn to read one time,' Ridelle said from the bunk. 'Don't have much time for book learning these days.'

'How d'you spell fight?' the sheriff asked.

'You mean as in fist fight or in gun play?' Vic Ridelle asked. He thought it best to keep this dumb sheriff in a sweet mood. That way he might break out of this dark cell that wasn't fit for a hog to sleep in.

'I mean in gun fight,' Stafford said.

'You mean like we had at that Scrambling Rocks place?' Keep him happy, keep the dumb cluck sweet. He won't know what hit him when it comes. 'You writing up your report?' he asked Stafford.

'That's no nevermind to you,' Stafford said over his shoulder. 'I write the goddamned truth, that's all.'

Though Ridelle was playing along as though he was treating the whole episode philosophically, he was feeling more than a little stirred up inside. What had happened up at the Scrambling Rocks had eaten right into his heart. He had pictured Horse Soldier swinging from a dead tree but now the picture had been ripped like a page from a scrapbook and he, Vic Ridelle, was the only one alive from the bunch. Except for Mingo and Mingo was a traitor beyond belief. If I had him here with a shooter in my hand, I'd empty a whole six slugs into his fat belly and teach him to do dirt on us like that!

Another voice whispered in his ear: 'Stay calm, man! Think about getting out of here and you might even keep that promise to yourself!'

*

137

Big Jim had dismounted again and he was a stooping over a pile of horse apples. 'Lookee here,' he said. 'It's still steaming. They can't be more than half a mile ahead.'

Horse Soldier checked his weapons and thought about Sarah riding with that great big bag of ordure. What has he done to her? he thought with horror.

That's not the point, man, a voice said inside his head. The point is you have to rescue her alive, you know that?

'Soon as we see them, what do you aim to do?' Big Jim said.

Horse Soldier had a picture in his mind. When he saw Mingo, he would just take his Winchester, aim it carefully and take Mingo out. In the picture Mingo would rise in the saddle, look round in amazement, and then drop down twitching on the ground.

'Lookee here,' Big Jim said, staring down at the tracks, 'one of those horses has gone lame.'

Horse Soldier dismounted and examined the tracks. 'Yeah,' he said. 'It was Morello's horse, the one Sarah was riding.' Now he was studying the other prints, those of his own horse that Mingo had taken. 'Just one good horse between them,' he said.

'It could be he left Sarah alone and rode on to escape,' Big Jim said. 'Had second thoughts about keeping her for himself.'

Horse Soldier thought about that and considered it to be most unlikely. Mingo must know his pursuers were catching up with him fast, though he wouldn't know how many of them there were. Mingo wasn't entirely stupid and he would have some tactic in mind.

Running Deer McVicar was sitting in the saloon, drinking

138

and having a meal – tough steak as usual. As a cook, Stan Balding's wife was about as good as a miner with a pickaxe and the steaks were just about the same.

Having returned from the Scrambling Rocks, Doc Higgins had given Morello and Running Deer the once over and pronounced them fit to go on living. The bullet that had hit Morello at an angle had left quite a gash that might turn septic but Running Deer's shoulder, though painful, had begun to heal well.

Running Deer was concerned about Morello, who, after all, had saved his life when Spike Ovenwood had bushwhacked him.

'So the doc thinks you gonna be all right?' Running Deer asked Morello.

Morello tried not to cough since coughing hurt him. 'I'm OK,' he said. 'I wear the armour of righteousness. Not so easy to kill.' He laughed and that made him cough.

'You gotta take care of yourself,' Running Deer advised.

Right at that moment Sheriff Stafford came into the saloon. He nodded to Running Deer and Morello and went over to the bar to speak to Stan Balding. 'That prisoner in the lock-up is asking for his chuck. Is it on its way?' Stafford felt somewhat demeaned at having to run errands for a prisoner, especially a desperate *hombre* like Ridelle, so he was intent on keeping his dignity. He had an arrangement with Stan Balding to feed any prisoners their meals, just as long as they weren't in the jail for too long which could be danged expensive.

Morello tried not to laugh again. 'Send him over one of your crack jaw steaks,' he said. 'That way he die before the hangman gets to put the rope around his neck.'

Everyone in the saloon laughed, except Running Deer, who took time off from gnawing at his steak to give the sheriff a suspicious look. 'You left that killer alone in the caboose?' he said.

'No harm in that,' Sheriff Stafford said. 'He's in his cell tight as a clam. Unless he's some kind of escape artist he isn't gonna get out of there.'

'You make bet?' Morello gave Running Deer an elaborate wink.

Sheriff Stafford snorted and left the saloon.

Stan Balding laughed and went through to talk to his wife, *the Butcher of Simm City.*

Running Deer wiped his mouth with the back of his hand and reached down for his Colt .45. He laid it on the table in front of him and checked the bullets in their chambers.

Morello said, 'You know, *amigo,* you lucky the bullet hit your left shoulder. You still draw gun and shoot. Defend yourself good, *sí?*'

Yes, and I should have been up there to smoke out that nest of rattlers, Running Deer thought. Firing a Colt with your left arm in a sling could be difficult, but he had practised in the yard behind the building and he knew he could still do it.

Now, having swallowed the last of his gristly steak he thought he would go out to the sidewalk and smoke a quirly. 'You roll me a quirly?' he said to Morello.

'Why, sure I roll.' Morello didn't approve of stinking the place out with tobacco but he would do anything to help his buddy. He had never smoked but he did chew a plug of tobacco now and then. So he understood Running Deer's need.

Running Deer accepted the quirly, examined it critically, lit it and stepped out on to the sidewalk to take a soothing smoke.

Sheriff Stafford was back in the jailhouse. He intended to work on his account of the Scrambling Rocks episode. He had begun to see himself as something of a literary figure. Somebody had to write these things down, and he was the man.

'Your chow is on its way,' he told the prisoner.

'Are they bringing rotgut too?' Ridelle enquired.

The sheriff chuckled. 'You don't get rotgut here,' he said, 'unless you can pay for it. If you're lucky they'll bring you that swill they call beer over there.'

'That's OK, Sheriff. I'll lay out for the rotgut.'

When the boy arrived with the tray of food covered with a cloth the sheriff ordered him to slide it under the bars of the cell. You don't want to let a prisoner like Ridelle get the drop on you, he thought.

Ridelle bent down to draw in the tray. Then he sniffed at his food. 'What do I do?' he asked wryly. 'Do I eat the tray, or what's on top of it?'

The boy and the sheriff laughed. No doubt they had both sampled Mrs Balding's cooking more than once!

'And bring me a bottle of that good hooch,' Vic Ridelle said to the boy, as he passed several dollar bills between the bars.

'Why, yes, *sir*!' said the boy.

Running Deer watched the boy coming and going across the street. 'Who are you serving, the Queen of Sheba?' he called out.

'No, sir, I'm taking food across to the prisoner,' the boy said. He wasn't too bright and he had never heard of the Queen of Sheba or any other queen if it came to that. He held up a dollar bill. 'He gave me good money, sir. Wants me to take him a bottle of whiskey.'

'He's going to need more than one bottle where he's going,' Running Deer said. The boy paused on the sidewalk. 'Is he the man who shot you in the shoulder, sir?'

'No, that was another *hombre*,' Running Deer replied.

'What happened to him?' the boy asked.

'Why, he's dead,' Running Deer said.

'Did Sheriff Stafford shoot him?' the boy asked, eager-eyed.

Running Deer didn't want to undermine the sheriff's authority, so he said, 'No, the guy who shot me was a little too gun happy and he got it from a guy called Mingo, so they say.'

That boy might not have been too bright but he liked to hang around and gossip. Running Deer figured he had caught that from his master, Stan Balding.

'Maybe you'd better fetch that hooch before the prisoner dies of thirst,' he said.

The boy gave a giggle and disappeared into the saloon.

Vic Ridelle had finished his steak. 'That steak was as tough as a mule-skinner's boot. I should have chosen ham and eggs,' he said.

Sheriff Stafford gave a superior chuckle. He was beginning to like Ridelle's sense of humour. A villain with a sense of humour was something he hadn't often come across.

'Are you writing your will?' Ridelle asked, from the

other side of the bars.

'Not yet,' Stafford said. 'I still have a little ways to go.'

'That's what a man thinks until his last hour,' Vic Ridelle said. 'Any chance I could take a leak around here?'

'Well, we don't encourage it, at least not in the cells,' the sheriff joked. 'The jakes is out there in the back.'

'Full of spiders and roaches, no doubt,' Ridelle surmised.

'The occasional rat too,' Stafford suggested.

Before they could pursue the topic further, the boy arrived with a bottle of Stan Balding's rather third-rate whiskey, probably watered down. Vic Ridelle uncorked it and took a sniff. Then he took a long swig from the bottle.

'You want to take a drink with me?' he said to Sheriff Stafford.

'Never drink on duty,' Stafford laughed. 'It's against the rules.'

'That so?' Ridelle said. 'Things are getting stricter every day.'

The boy was giggling. He couldn't believe what they had told him about Ridelle. He knew Clemy and Sarah and he couldn't believe anyone would want to kidnap them. He had seen Horse Soldier too, and he was much more of a hard-faced dude than Ridelle!

Now, Sheriff Stafford had drawn his gun and levelled it at Ridelle. 'Take the keys and unlock the door of the cell,' he said to the boy. 'The man wants to take a leak.'

The boy fumbled with the keys but couldn't find the right one.

'It's this one,' Stafford said, selecting the appropriate key.

The boy hadn't unlocked the cell door before and no

doubt he felt privileged. Maybe later he would be depu-
tized or he might even be sworn in as sheriff some day.

Ridelle stepped out of the cell and flexed his arms.
'That's better,' he said. 'A man feels a little safer out here.
Lead the way to that wonderful hole in the ground you
mentioned. Those roaches and rats are in for a treat.'

Sheriff Stafford was still chuckling to himself as he
showed Ridelle through to the jakes. Ridelle was still
taking swigs from his bottle.

Running Deer was sitting out there on the sidewalk trying
to digest his indigestible steak when he heard a muffled
shot. The next moment the boy burst out of the jailhouse
and came half staggering towards him. 'He shot the
sheriff!' the boy said aghast. 'That man shot the sheriff!'
He stared at Running Deer as though he couldn't believe
it.

Running Deer was already on his feet with his Colt in
his hand. Then he heard a second shot and Vic Ridelle
lurched out of the jailhouse with a smoking gun.

Ridelle had been in the jakes doing his business and
taking swigs from the whiskey bottle. He had said to
Stafford, 'Ain't there an ounce of decency around here? A
man can't take a leak and something else without people
looking on?'

Sheriff Stafford had obligingly half closed the door.

When Ridelle emerged saying, 'That was some relief,
Sheriff. I really needed it and it sure scared the shits out of
those rats!'

Stafford laughed and lowered the Colt and that was his
last big mistake. The next instant he took a large glug of

whiskey right in the eyes. Then he felt a fist smack into his jaw, followed by a knee crashing into his groin. His brain exploded in a maze of flashing stars.

Ridelle stooped and retrieved the sheriff's Colt. Then he shot Stafford full in the chest.

'You dumb cluck lawman!' he shouted. 'You think you can keep a man like me in your rat-infested jail, think again!'

Then he shot the dying man right through the head. Sheriff Stafford's head jerked up from the jailhouse floor and then fell back. His mouth was open as though he wanted to say something but all that came out was a gurgle of death.

The boy had seen all this from the door but he didn't wait for a third shot. That was when he leaped over the sidewalk and ran furiously towards the saloon.

Running Deer McVicar stepped on to Main Street and saw Vic Ridelle grabbing a horse from the hitching rail. The next instant the kidnapper and killer would be astride that horse and riding hell for leather out of town. Not a soul could stop him. *Except me,* thought Running Deer.

All the frustration of the last days boiled up in him suddenly. 'Stay where you are, and drop that gun!' he shouted.

Ridelle turned on Main Street and fired a shot at Running Deer. The bullet missed and shattered a window pane of the saloon.

Running Deer held his Colt, steadied it, and fired a shot.

Ridelle lurched but didn't fall. Now he was behind the horse ready to leap up on to its back. He turned in the

saddle and fired another shot in Running Deer's direction, but now the horse was rearing up and the shot
missed.

'Two more left!' Running Deer said to himself.

He raised his gun and fired again.

Now Ridelle was in the saddle and there was no stop-
ping him. 'He's getting away!' someone said from close by.
It was Morello who, despite his wound, had managed to
stagger out of the saloon.

'Don't worry,' Running Deer said. 'I hit him. He won't
get far.'

They watched as Ridelle rode away, but not for more
than fifty yards when he slid down from the saddle and fell
and the spooked horse galloped on.

Running Deer took his time. He walked quite leisurely
over to Ridelle who was breathing hard from the tumble
he had taken, but he still had the strength to raise his gun.

'You've got two slugs left,' Running Deer told him.
'Only two slugs. You better make them count.'

Ridelle's hand was trembling as he steadied the gun
and fired.

Running Deer knelt down close and leered into his
face. 'You killed my pa and held that girl and her ma prisoner. Now you get what's coming to you, you low-down
skunk!'

Ridelle had one shot left and he made a supreme effort
but it was just too much for him. The bullet passed harmlessly into the sky and Ridelle shuddered and died.

'Those who live by the sword shall die by the sword,'
Morello said like an ancient prophet.

'Amen to that,' Running Deer replied.

'Amen,' echoed a whole a bunch of people who had

emerged from close by to witness Vic Ridelle's demise.

Horse Soldier and Big Jim rode on until they came to Sarah's mount limping on the trail. Horse dismounted and took the horse by the reins. 'There, there, old buddy,' he said. 'Did my wife Sarah give you a message for me?'

Big Jim was surprised. He had seen *hombres* talk to horses before but most of them were plumb loco and Horse Soldier was one of the sanest people he had met.

'That's real bad,' Mingo said. He had made Sarah dismount from the horse and take down the saddle-bag. Then he got down from Horse Soldier's horse and pointed the shooter at Sarah. 'Now you do as I bid and you're gonna survive,' he said.

'The only thing you can do is let me go free,' Sarah said defiantly. 'Horse Soldier will catch up with us soon, and if you ride on you might just escape.'

But Mingo levelled the gun at her. 'You've got sand, I'll give you that. I admire a woman with sand in her craw. What I want for you to do is mount up in front of me and we ride along together. Your old man isn't going to shoot at us in case he kills you as well as me. Have you thought of that?'

'I see things differently,' Sarah replied. 'If we ride on together on the same horse we won't get far. Too much weight for the horse to bear.'

That was true and Mingo knew it. He was determined to keep his prize for as long as he could. 'Like I told you, that bounty hunter is no use to any woman.'

'Whereas you are a true blue, gold-star husband for any woman,' Sarah said with more than a tinge of irony.

'Now you just mount up in front of me like I said,' Mingo ordered, brandishing his gun.

The thought of riding in front of Mingo with the stink of his sweat in her nostrils and the feel of his huge arms around her waist made Sarah want to throw up.

'You want to shoot me, shoot me now!' she said defiantly.

Mingo shrugged his shoulders. Maybe at that moment he should have ridden on, but he was as stubborn as a mule and stiff necked as a winter scarecrow and he knew what he wanted. 'I made a deal with your man Horse,' he said. 'I promised him I'd save you from those desperate killers and he said he'd pay me a handsome price.'

'Well, maybe he will and maybe he won't,' she said. 'You wait here long enough, you'll find out.' It was the first she had heard of any deal between Mingo and her husband.

Horse Soldier threw up his arm and he and Big Jim reined in and listened. They heard voices not far ahead.

'That's Sarah,' Horse said, 'and she's trying to talk sense into that lump of buffalo meat.'

Big Jim narrowed his eyes and peered ahead. 'I think I see them,' he said.

Horse saw them too. They were standing together. Mingo had his gun levelled at Sarah and Sarah was standing up to him and arguing with him. Sarah is no shrinking violet, he thought proudly.

'We shoot now we might bring them both down,' Big Jim said.

'I think we don't shoot,' Horse said. 'If it comes to shooting I'm gonna be the one to take that gorilla into the next world for good or bad.'

Big Jim shrugged his slender shoulders. 'Two guns are better than one,' he said philosophically.

Horse touched the sides of his mount and he and Big Jim rode forward together.

Mingo and Sarah were in the middle of a scrubby clearing when they heard Horse Soldier and Big Jim approaching.

'You want to stay alive, don't do anything foolish,' Sarah said to Mingo. At that moment she saw anger and cunning wrestling like Jacob and the Angel in Mingo's brain.

Then Mingo reached out and grabbed her round her neck and held her to him and she caught the reek of his sweat in her nostrils. It was the stink of fear and treachery.

He dragged her behind the horse, keeping it between Horse Soldier and himself.

'Why, Horse Soldier!' he shouted. 'You got here just about in time! I promised you I'd rescue your woman from those killers, didn't I? We made a deal, remember?'

'I remember it well!' Horse Soldier shouted. 'You killed one of those crazy men and then rode away with Sarah. That wasn't part of the deal, was it?'

Mingo shook his head. 'Heat of the moment,' he said. 'Seemed the best thing to do at the time.'

'So why am I tracking you down like this?' Horse Soldier sang out.

Big Jim was fingering his shooter. 'He's trying to spin out time to fool you,' he said. 'He aims to ride off with your wife in his pocket. You want me to get on the other side of him and blast him down?'

'Like I told you,' Horse said, 'if someone has to kill that big ape it's gonna be me.' He jigged his horse and edged on towards Mingo and Sarah.

'Stay where you are!' Mingo warned. 'I don't want to have to kill this sweet woman.' Now he had his arm round Sarah's throat and a gun at her temple. 'But I will, if I have to.' He had moved away from the horse, so they were now fully exposed.

'What do you want, Mingo?' Horse Soldier sang out, trying to sound steady and reasonable.

'I want you to get off your horse, lay your gun on the ground and tell that sidekick you got with you to do the same. Then we can talk sense,' Mingo replied.

'Do as the man says,' Horse said to Big Jim out of the corner of his mouth.

Big Jim growled with frustration and dismounted.

'That's right,' Mingo said. 'Now you both come forward with your hands in the air and we can parley.'

'Like a lamb to the slaughter,' Jim grumbled as they stepped forward.

Horse Soldier and Big Jim had their hands raised.

'Now all he has to do is shoot us both and that's his happy ending,' Big Jim said. He didn't sound too happy about the prospect but his voice was steady.

Mingo took his gun off Sarah's temple and trained it on Horse Soldier. 'Now just stay where you are,' he said. 'And you, little man, I want for you to bring me the best of those two flea-bitten nags so the lady can ride on with dignity.'

'Do as the man says,' Horse Soldier said quietly to Big Jim.

Big Jim gave a curt nod and walked back to the two horses.

'Bring me the grey!' Mingo shouted. 'Looks just dandy for a lady.' He tightened his grip on Sarah's throat and waved the gun in Horse Soldier's direction. 'Nice piece of horse flesh you got here,' he said, referring to Horse Soldier's animal which he had been riding. 'Seems fitting, don't it, me riding away with your woman on your horse; But maybe you're not gonna need either of them, after all.' He gave a growl of laughter like those sinister thunderheads.

Horse Soldier was looking at Sarah, trying to read her expression. He saw that she was terrified but that she was trying to work out her next move. 'What do you want me to do?' her eyes seemed to say.

Big Jim took the grey and led it towards Mingo and Sarah.

Horse could see that Mingo had a difficulty. He couldn't get Sarah on to the horse without releasing her and, when he released her, he would leave himself open.

'Now, mount up, lady,' Mingo said.

Horse could see that this was Sarah's chance to make her move. Mingo had the reins of Sarah's intended mount in his left hand and his gun in his right. She was about to swing into the saddle of her intended, so-called 'flea bitten nag'. She was an excellent horsewoman and could have ridden in a circus.

Horse Soldier knew by telepathy what was coming. He gave a high whistle and his own horse, lurched towards him. Sarah instantly kicked out sideways at Mingo's head. Her foot caught him a glancing blow and it was enough to deflected his attention. He fired a shot but the bullet went wide.

Horse Soldier darted forward and made a giant leap which sent the big man sprawling backwards. The next moment Mingo took the heel of Horse Soldier's boot right on the jaw.

Sarah pulled her horse sideways and Big Jim made a dive for his discarded gunbelt and yanked out his Colt.

Mingo had somehow managed to retain his grip on his gun but his eyes were covered with blood. He loosed off another shot which also went wide.

Horse Soldier came in with another kick as Mingo struggled to get to his feet.

Big Jim ran in with his gun but he couldn't do a thing. Horse Soldier was on the big man, pummelling him right and left with his fists. Mingo was big but he was more nimble than he looked. He managed to roll away and make a grab for his lost gun.

Now Big Jim ran in to cover him. 'You move another inch and you'll be dead meat!' he cried.

Mingo glared at him, snorting and breathing wildly.

Horse Soldier gathered up Mingo's gun and struggled to his feet.

'Now get yourself up, you lousy bag of blubber!' Big Jim said.

Mingo grunted and they watched him struggling to get on to his feet.

Mingo stood shaking and snorting and trying to recover his breath. As his breathing began to quieten, they saw something like dignity return to his demeanour. He wiped the blood and sweat away from his face with his sleeve. 'You guys got a quirly for a man?" he asked, looking at Big Jim.

'No more tricks,' Big Jim said as he produced a tobacco pouch, rolled a cigarette, struck a light, and handed it to Mingo.

Mingo sucked on it for a moment. 'What happens next?' he asked.

'I guess that's your last smoke, Mingo,' Big Jim said. 'Now we string you up from that stunted tree over there and leave you hanging there for the buzzards to tear to pieces with their beaks and talons.'

Mingo nodded and looked at Horse Soldier. 'Are you the judge and jury?' he asked him.

Horse Soldier grinned and nodded. 'You're your own judge and jury,' he replied. 'You stepped a little too far on this one, Mingo, and you've got to live or die with what you did.'

Now Sarah dismounted and she stood regarding Mingo. Despite all the grime and wear and tear of the last days she was still a very handsome woman. 'You've put me through hell and highwater,' she said to Mingo.

'Well, I can only apologize for that, lady,' Mingo said. 'At least you're back with your husband now. I never meant for you no harm, anyway.' He turned to Horse Soldier and grinned through his blood-matted beard. 'I thought we made a deal. I kept my part of the bargain. You promised me a poke. Now you're going to hang me.'

Horse Soldier held his head on one side. 'Like I told you, Mingo, you double-crossed me, but I'm no hanging judge. We could take you back to Simm City and wait for the judge and leave it for him to decide.' He sucked on his teeth for a moment. 'But I don't aim to do that.'

An expression of bewilderment and dawned on Mlngo's visage. 'What do you aim to do then?' he asked.

'Well, now,' Horse Soldier reflected. 'In old times, so they tell me, they used to pick out a ram and load it with people's sins and send it out into the wilderness.'

'I thought they just slit its throat?' Big Jim said.

'I believe they sometimes did that too,' Horse Soldier agreed. 'It's a question of balancing revenge and mercy and I'm inclined to go for mercy. Revenge never did anybody any good.'

Big Jim gave a snort of disgust. 'You think this lump of decay deserves mercy?' he said.

Horse Soldier looked at Sarah. 'What do you think?' he asked her.

Sarah switched to Mingo and gave him a long hard look. 'I choose mercy,' she said.

Horse Soldier smiled. 'Then that's the ace card, Mingo. We choose mercy, but it's gonna be a hard road. What we do is give you that *flea-bitten grey horse* you had in mind for Sarah and you can ride away a free man . . . on one condition.'

Mingo looked at Horse Soldier and then at Sarah, but Sarah was looking at Horse with a grim smile.

Horse Soldier took a step closer to Mingo and pointed his gun at his bloody beard. 'And this is the condition: if I see you again, Mingo, I'm gonna shoot you dead. No messing, no excuses, no ifs and buts. You understand that?'

'Amen to that,' Big Jim said.

Mingo shrugged and nodded. 'That's not a bad deal for a bounty hunter,' he said. He shrugged his broad shoulders. Then he retrieved his somewhat battered Stetson, mounted the grey, gave Sarah one last look, and rode off, no doubt a relieved but disappointed man.

CHAPTER TEN

The first person to see Sarah and Horse Soldier was young Clementine. Clemy had been in agony since she got back to the ranch. Of course, Phoebe Potkin had taken good care of her, but Phoebe, though a woman with a warm heart and good intentions, was something of a nag. Ed Potkin, her husband, was usually at the receiving end of her diatribes, especially since he had nearly got himself killed with Horse Soldier. What was the use of a man who couldn't do what was needed around the place? A woman couldn't be expected to do everything, could she?

Phoebe was fond of Sarah and she worried about her constantly. Sarah was a steady young woman and an excellent friend and neighbour. Where could she be now, Phoebe wondered, and what would happen to Clemy if she lost Sarah and Horse Soldier? What a name to call a man! Phoebe thought. A man who was so seldom at home too! Phoebe had never approved of Horse Soldier and she thought her old fool of a husband had been led by the nose by him. Now she had so much work on her hands because of Horse Soldier and her numbskull of a husband who was so easily led! And so on . . . and so forth. . . .

Phoebe was mumbling to herself on these lines when Clemy came rushing over to her. 'Aunt Phoebe!' she cried. 'They're coming, Aunt Phoebe, I've seen them! My ma and pa are here!'

They stood together and watched as Sarah and Horse Soldier and Big Jim came riding towards them from the direction of the bluff. Sarah was waving and shouting.

Clemy gave a cheer as she rushed excitedly to meet them.

Ed Potkin came out of the cabin. For some reason he felt redeemed and he wanted to say to Phoebe, 'Look, what did I tell you! They're alive and Sarah's free!'

They watched as Sarah urged her horse forward and came in at a gallop.

Horse Soldier was leading the lame horse, so he rode a little more slowly. Big Jim didn't wave but he too looked pleased. He was tempted to draw his shooter and loose off a couple of celebratory shots!

That was some reunion especially as Doc Higgins came riding in about half an hour later to check on Ed and Clemy and also to sample some of Phoebe's excellent cooking on the side. Doc Higgins could always depend on receiving a good meal wherever he went. It was mostly from him that Sarah and Horse Soldier learned of the events in Simm City, how Vic Ridelle had shot Sheriff Stafford to death and how Running Deer had shot Ridelle before he could escape.

Nobody had much time for Stafford as sheriff but, as a man, he had been greatly respected especially in the Balding saloon, his usual hang-out. He and Doc Higgins had been friends and that was enough for the community.

Anybody who was friendly with the doc must have a lot of good in him. So the community was in deep mourning for Sheriff Stafford who would be given the best funeral that Simm City could afford.

Doc Higgins was concerned about Clemy. She was brave and gutsy, but what effect would these dire events have on her mind? She had seen men killed; she had been kid-napped and threatened; she had made her escape, leaving her mother behind. Those events could scar a girl for life.

In fact, Clemy had become something of a heroine at the Simm City school. The children had never believed that Clemy had been on holiday as Mrs Beardmore alleged. They took a different view especially after the shootings at the jail. One boy who always knew everything, claimed to have seen Vic Ridelle's body lying stretched out on Main Street with bullet holes all over his chest. Ridelle had even fired a shot in the boy's direction before he died, but the boy had dodged behind a water-barrel and avoided the bullet.

Most of the kids had heard Harry Jessop's tall stories before so they weren't unduly impressed. On the other hand Clemy Millar had actually been kidnapped and *she had made her escape*! That was something for the record books, wasn't it? And she looked such a normal kid, too!

'How did you get away, Clemy?' one of her friends asked wide-eyed.

'Did you actually shoot those kidnappers?' another pupil asked.

'Is your pa a real gunman?' one of the more daring boys asked.

'Why is he called Horse Soldier?' another inquisitive

pupil enquired.

'Now, children,' Mrs Beardmore intervened, 'We have
work to do. Get back to your desks and your slates.
Clementine needs to rest. You'll wear her out with all your
questioning.'

Sarah wasn't so lucky. For some days after the ordeal she
couldn't sleep. She kept seeing a huge monster with red
blazing eyes and breath that reeked of rotting corpses and
it groped towards her through a forest of dark trees with
tendrils that encircled her ankles and dragged her down
into choking mud. And Sarah woke screaming in panic.

'Hush, baby,' came the voice of the Archangel Raphael.
'Hush, baby, you're safe.' But it wasn't the archangel but
her husband who spoke in a quiet and gentle tone.

Horse Soldier! What a name for a man! she had often
thought. But now she was glad. He was as brave as a soldier
and he loved to ride. He was fierce and relentless, but as
gentle as a dove too. Sarah needed that gentleness and
understanding, and she slept happily again.

Now as winter drew close Running Deer came to the
house with Morello and Big Jim.

Morello had healed well and he was full of praise for
the divine powers that had helped Doc Higgins to make
him whole again. 'We stay in Simm City till the spring-
time,' he said. 'Then my *amigo* and me go to the *ranchito*
and work.'

Big Jim nodded. 'Little spread over Vegas way. A buddy
of mine is the ramrod there.'

'You got money?' Horse Soldier asked.

'Sure, we got enough,' Big Jim said. 'We did a deal with

Stan Balding. Only thing is his wife needs to take cooking lessons. If she worked on a ranch the hands would vamoose inside of a week. If it ain't teeth-grinding steak it's son-of-a-bitch stew.'

Morello gave a cackling chuckle.

Running Deer was less communicative. Now that the *hombres* who had killed his pa had been executed, he didn't know what to do. Revenge was sweet, but maybe not quite as sweet as he had expected. He was still smouldering inside because Horse Soldier had let Mingo go free. 'You knew that big guy was a killer like all the rest. He might not have been in on my pa's killing but he went along with the kidnapping, didn't he?'

There was no arguing with that. So Horse changed the subject. 'What will you do now?' he asked.

Running Deer frowned. 'I don't rightly know. I could put in to be sheriff of Simm City if I have a mind to it. Doc Higgins reckons I have the necessary qualifications. Not much money but it's steady, after all.'

Horse Soldier became more and and more restless as winter came and the bleak gales swept across the prairie. Ferrying Clemy to school was often a problem but, except for the bleakest of times when the trail was impassable, they didn't miss a day. In the depths of winter he piled logs on the fire and taught her himself. Horse wasn't gifted as a teacher and quite often Sarah needed to correct him on points of grammar and calculation. Sarah was patient and kind and Clemy blossomed under her guidance.

Some evenings Phoebe and Ed Potkins would come up for supper. As the months drew on Phoebe mellowed somewhat, especially after Ed went down with the flu and she thought she was going to lose him.

Phoebe and Sarah would yarn together as they collaborated in the cooking and Clemy joined in too. That terrible episode had a silver lining and Clemy was blossoming into a fine intelligent young woman.

Ed and Horse sat together beside the blazing hearth. Ed smoked his pipe contentedly, reminiscing about the old times when he had been an army scout. 'Them Comanches were something else again,' he said. 'I learned to have a powerful respect for those short bowlegged men with their long lances. Nobody could beat them on the plains and nobody could ride like them either. Not even the Apache. But the Apache had their own qualities. Best skirmishers I ever met.'

He puffed away at his pipe for a moment and then said, somewhat mischievously, 'Sometimes I have a hankering for those old days, you know. You never knew whether your scalp was safe but by Gawd you certainly knew you were alive!'

He laughed and puffed away contentedly again.

'You know, I can't see you as a farmer, Horse. You got too much grit. Now what have you in mind to do next? That's what I'd like to know.'

Horse Soldier stared at the dancing flames for a while. He could hear Sarah and Phoebe laughing together by the stove. And then he heard Clemy joining in.

'I don't know,' he said. 'I can't read the stars but I guess something will turn up.'